My Dragon Mother

The Dragon's Cup

By Arturo Huerta

First Edition

Imagine Nation
www.ImagineNation.ws

Copyright © 2011 Arturo Huerta.

All rights reserved. Published by Imagine Nation. No part of this publication may be reproduced, stored in any data retrieval system, or transmitted in any form or by any means, electronic, mechanical, photocopying, recording, or otherwise, without the express written consent of the publisher, except in the case of brief quotations embodied in critical articles or reviews.

This is a work of fiction. All names, characters, places, and incidents are either the product of the author's imagination or are used fictitiously. Any resemblance to actual persons, living or dead, business establishments, events, or locales is purely coincidental.

All characters, character names, and the distinctive likenesses thereof are the property of Imagine Nation.

Cover Concept by Zara Sharaf Huerta
Illustrated by Jean Pe

Library of Congress Control Number: 2011939145
ISBN-13: 978-0615540931
ISBN-10: 0615540937

www.ImagineNation.ws

Dedication

For my lovely daughter, Zara.

Acknowledgement

Special thanks to my beautiful wife,
who inspired me to write . . .
then edit, and write again.

And to my loving parents
for their continued support
and encouragement.

Table of Contents

Family Ties 1

Who Are You? 16

A Family, A Home 30

A Shield for a Sword 49

The Search 67

The New Boy 85

Having Fun 99

A Celebration 116

The Plan 132

A Beautiful Place 150

The Storm Within 163

Dark Tidings 178

Mother's Milk 195

~ My Dragon Mother: The Dragon's Cup ~

Chapter I

Family Ties

"Why does the sun insist on resting?" mutters Ernust, a tall, wiry figure stumbling through the cold dark wood.

He is tired -- not just from running, but of living in his meager condition. His muscles ache from the beating he has endured from both land and fists, yet he continues to trudge, knowing that his goal nears with every painful step.

~ My Dragon Mother: The Dragon's Cup ~

Suddenly, a woman screams in the distance under the thunderous stampede of a soldier's horse. Ernust runs to save her, but arrives just in time to see her assailant flee.

Holding her head in his hand, the anxious man feels her warm blood trickling down his forearm. As he shifts his position, the woman closes her eyes, fades, and then vanishes, leaving the disturbed figure to his morbid delusion.

Ernust shakes his head frantically, trying to stop the subsequent flashes of violence that plague his tormented mind. Visions or memories, he is unable to distinguish between them. All he knows is that they are fresh from the night before.

At least now . . . there is no harried chase, nor imminent fear of capture; but rather a frenzied sense of urgency to get away from the dire circumstances surrounding his miserable existence.

It has been a long journey with little light, even less rest, and absolutely no indication of how far he has travelled. All he knows is that the land is now completely foreign, a good sign that he is moving further away from what is truly a dreary

~ Family Ties ~

place.

The hunched man stops for a brief moment to rub his lower back, gazing wearily at yet another steep hill on the path ahead of him. As Ernust starts his ascent, his mind flashes with another wave of cruel memories, offering no solace amid these dark surroundings.

He continues moving his feet, one mindless foot in front of the other, in a blind sense of faith that the sun will somehow let him know when he can finally rest.

It is now early morning, but with covered skies still wringing the last bit of rain from the night before, the coming dawn is barely worth noting.

"That was close," he gasps, falling to his knee as he slips on yet another root.

The gloomy forest continues to be unkind to him; offering only scrapes, bruises, and fearsome images as lasting mementoes of its passage.

Yet, he holds on to his parcel, the most prized of his possessions -- never once letting it make contact with the ground. Ernust checks to make sure everything is intact and continues to advance across the mud and moss that lay ahead.

"These are hard times," he thinks to himself as he struggles past a series of outstretched branches.

Once again, the limbs of the trees are unbending, giving him little aid in navigating the dark wet terrain. He finally breaks through their stiff grasp, splintering the black skeletal fingers that futilely tried to contain him.

As Ernust assesses his progress, he reflects on how radically his life had recently changed. Where he was once blessed with a beautiful home, he now finds himself destitute among the outskirts of society. Indeed, these were more than just hard times -- they were the darkest days he had ever known.

He reflects on when the rumors first started . . . when the Barons began to yearn for more than they had already been given. It seemed almost overnight that they started fighting amongst themselves to control each other's lands.

At first, their campaigns were merely wars of words, yielding little more than a spree of arranged

~ Family Ties ~

marriages that peacefully bound reluctant neighbors.

Then . . . there was fire.

No longer content to rule their traditional and adjacent provinces, the Barons entered into fierce battles with clans beyond their immediate sights.

The worst among them was King Meinrad of the Black Forest, a cold-hearted tyrant intent on ruling a land without borders.

He was as cruel as he was cunning, laying waste to anyone who did not immediately acknowledge his supremacy.

In his voracious quest for power, his heart and mind became corrupt to the point where he increasingly favored property in lieu of life. This became apparent in the manner in which he decimated entire villages and further subjugated the few surviving inhabitants.

He sent armies to burn the region around his own, sparing only those who pledged their loyalty and vowed to pay him tribute. Otherwise, his legion was encouraged to pillage the land and rob its inhabitants of their remaining dignity.

~ My Dragon Mother: The Dragon's Cup ~

Countless acres of crops and woods were scorched, leaving hunger where there need not be any. Thus began the cycle of misery among both man and beast, affecting all who had a relationship with the living.

"This is far enough," mumbles Ernust as he opens the delicate package that lay in his aching arms.

There is a barely audible yawn as an infant stretches his arms and legs beyond the damp rags that dress him.

The child is hardly a few weeks old and is already malnourished, as evident by his unusually scrawny appearance. With dark circles under his eyes and not a hint of fat beneath his hollow cheeks, the child's weakened state was unmistakable.

Finally awake, he gazes into his father's eyes; feeling the warmth, strength, and security of his firm grasp.

Ernust smiles at his son and cradles him on his forearm, gently stroking the soft, gray skin on the child's arms and face.

The young boy squints as he feels the gentle

~ Family Ties ~

scratching of his father's touch upon his cheek.

His were laborer's hands -- rough and sturdy as the ground he tended. Yet also nurturing -- prompting life where none had existed prior.

At least, until yesterday . . . when Meinrad's men pressed firmly for his allegiance.

Ernust was a simple man who was not the least bit interested in politics. He sought only to provide for his family and insisted on remaining neutral in the affairs of the ruling class.

He assured Meinrad's soldiers that he would pay the required tribute and not cause trouble for the emerging regime. However, he could not, in good conscience, swear loyalty to a man who so blatantly disregarded the sanctity of life.

Ernust closes his eyes as he feels pangs of regret for having uttered those final words. For in this single act of defiance, the king's emissary deemed the farmer's behavior to be thoroughly unacceptable.

He declared the King had been insulted and ordered his men to destroy Ernust's home, burn his crop, and trample his beloved wife as payment for his insolence.

Ernust's pale, charred hands once again quiver with the fresh memory of his wife's horrific death. As he peers through the film of his grief-stricken eyes, he refocuses his thoughts and observes a well worn path in the distance . . . One with more signs of traffic than any before it.

A single ray of sunlight penetrates the clouds, illuminating a large stone at the path's center. At last, this is the sign that he had been waiting for.

As he walks towards the sunny stone, a warm breeze brushes his face like the caress of a consoling friend, reassuring him of his intent.

"This is a good spot," he whispers to himself. "I'll bet many travelers pass through here. Hopefully one of them will open his heart and take you far from this dreadful place."

Ernust pauses briefly to reconsider his actions. He shakes his head in disbelief and finally stares deeply at his infant son in a solemn, silent farewell.

Then, with a haggard appearance and defeated

~ Family Ties ~

spirit, Ernust props up his only child so that any passersby may readily see him and not run him over with their horses or carriages.

He places the boy onto the road, wondering aloud about the safety of his child.

"Should I place him on the side or in the middle?" he thinks to himself. "How long will it be before someone passes? What if they don't see him? Surely he will die."

Ernust pats down the boy's dark brown hair and wipes away the soot from his cheeks in a harried attempt to make him more presentable. He then adjusts the child's rags to provide for a soft cushion against the unforgiving, lump-ridden ground.

Calm and content, the child's comfort and safety are quickly doused as his father turns his back to him for the first and final time. As Ernust walks away, the day breaks through the clouds just as the silence is broken with the cries of his infant son.

The tormented father shuts his eyes in a failed attempt to block out his son's wailing sounds and continues to march homeward with bitter resolve.

~ My Dragon Mother: The Dragon's Cup ~

The child's cries grow fainter in the distance until he can only hear them in his conscience.

***

Darkness falls and the night forest teems with the flutter, screech, and growl of a living wood. Snapping twigs and rustling leaves serve mainly to heighten the stifling anxiety already felt in such alien terrain.

The evening temperature drops quickly as mere moonbeams offer little warmth when compared to the nurturing rays of the life-giving sun.

The deserted infant grows tired and hungry, looking for signs of his parents without success. His previously unfailing signs of safety and comfort have all simply vanished with no sign of returning any time soon.

As he scans the gloomy landscape, he realizes that for the very first time in his tiny life . . . he is completely alone.

With the passing of his father's footsteps, the unfamiliar sounds of the forest grow increasingly louder until the lone child is fully engulfed with the

~ Family Ties ~

frenzy of life itself.

At once, he appreciates the enormity and complexity of the world and how truly helpless he is at present. With this unsettling knowledge, he begins to cry, drawing the unwanted attention of all sorts of creatures in the dark.

His screams continue through the night, yet he gains only the burning sensation of a strained throat. Sadly, it is his only source of warmth, so he resumes his act of futility once more.

All of a sudden, the constant trickle of tears down his grief-ridden face is disrupted by a curious flickering in the midnight sky.

The infant child notices a strange shadow passing back and forth, blocking the crescent moon overhead. Its rhythm is hypnotic in how it slows in cycle but grows in duration with each additional passage.

The boy is stunned into silence as he tries to distinguish the peculiar shape of the approaching figure. He had never seen anything like it before and begins to wonder what it could possibly be and

~ My Dragon Mother: The Dragon's Cup ~

whether it would harm him.

For now, all he knows for certain is that the shadow is drawing ever closer with each additional pass.

Before long, he feels a cool breeze -- emanating not from the hills or valleys, but rather from the sky above, as if being pushed down upon him like a summer rain.

The towering firs and pines around him shake frantically, with some even crackling, as the unusual shadow physically touches the ground, resulting in a deep and muffled thump.

Suddenly, the night sky is thoroughly consumed by the dark mysterious figure to where the slightest glimmer of light is no longer visible, even through the corners of the child's hazelnut eyes.

The twinkling stars and shining moon are instead replaced by a pair of jagged emeralds and long pointed fangs slightly illuminated with the intermittent flicker of hellish amber flame.

The child's eyes widen in panic as he gasps for what is likely to be his final breath. Like any other

~ Family Ties ~

child, he had previously known fear, but never to the level of terror as he had experienced on this fateful night.

The towering beast observes the child, swaying back and forth in the process, like a serpent sizing up its helpless victim. With each rhythmic motion, its scales reflect the scant amount of shifting light into a series of dark waves splashing across its colossal figure.

The ominous giant then raises its left arm into the air and with a single swift motion, scoops the paralyzed infant into one of its massive, tent-like wings.

The child flies high into the air, leaving the familiarity of the large stone that had accompanied it by the roadside.

The terrifying beast then proceeds to break off the end of its right talon, wincing in pain as it rips off the remaining tissue. It then uses the freshly-torn claw to gently scratch at the young boy's tender chapped lips.

The little boy tries desperately in vain to

wrestle away from the menacing creature. He turns in an effort to spot a more tranquil setting, a sort of last request for the condemned.

Ultimately, the creature's giant claw proves to be successful and pries open the young boy's toothless mouth, making its way well past both tongue and cheek.

With his jaws completely immobilized, the young boy struggles to regain his breath. He then begins to feel a surge of warm liquid flowing past his lips . . . something he immediately recognizes -- Milk!

At once, the boy feels a sense of relief as he now comes to realize that he is being fed rather than being fed upon.

Given their immense size difference, the mammoth beast had used its own claw as an improvised funnel to feed the debilitated infant.

The child is frantic with hunger and hastily swallows the familiar soothing beverage, forgetting to pause between gulps.

He coughs until he catches his breath, spilling the beast's wholesome milk onto the ground below.

~ Family Ties ~

Unable to resist the rushing flood, he drinks until his belly is full and falls fast asleep.

As his eyes begin to close, a bright light radiates from beneath his sleepy eyelids, faintly illuminating their immediate surroundings.

He reaches out blindly towards the creature, latching firmly onto its broken talon. He gently wraps his scrawny fingers around it, silently expressing gratitude for its care.

Finally, he fades into unconsciousness just as the shimmering glow from his eyes is extinguished, reverting the backdrop into its original state of darkness.

~ My Dragon Mother: The Dragon's Cup ~

Chapter II

Who Are You?

Fully rested, the young child awakens late in the day unable to determine how much time had already passed. He surveys the terrain only to perceive a supernatural realm unlike the house or hills that he had previously known.

The little boy is confounded by the mystical cavern in which he finds himself, where the floor and walls are encrusted with glistening jewels that are smooth and warm to the touch.

~ Who Are You? ~

There is no river, or lake, or even mountains as he had previously remembered. Rather it appears to be more of a bejeweled cage, where even the shifting sun is no longer visible.

Focusing back on himself, he feels different than before -- bigger and stronger than he had ever experienced. He sits up for the first time ever and incredibly stretches his arms and legs well beyond the length to which he had been accustomed.

"Thump!" echoes his ankle as it lands upon the soft ground beneath it.

"What happened to me?" he wonders, lifting his arms and legs once more.

Frightened yet excited, he examines his more muscular hands and feet, flexing them as he had never done previously.

"Should I try to stand?" he asks himself. "What if I fall?"

Encouraged by his strapping posture, the young boy rises tentatively to a standing position, while at the same time fashioning his tattered rags into makeshift clothing.

~ My Dragon Mother: The Dragon's Cup ~

With his new perspective, he again observes his strange surroundings and mumbles, "Where am I?"

"You are safe," replies a soft voice in a reassuring whisper.

Shocked by the unexpected response, the frightened child turns anxiously to identify the anonymous speaker, though none was to be found. He looks to see if perhaps a corner of the small room would reveal an opening, but again nothing else came into view.

"Am I . . . dead?" he stammers in a low trembling tone, not knowing for certain whether he really wanted to know the answer to his momentous question.

"In a way, yes . . . but not as you would expect," the faceless voice replies, fading again into the distant background.

The boy ponders the mysterious comment, but is unable to decipher it.

"What is your name?" the voice continues from what appears to be in every direction.

~ Who Are You? ~

"I . . . don't have one," the child mutters with a hung head, feeling ashamed for having been abandoned.

By uttering those words, the young boy realizes that in addition to being nameless, he also has no sense of identity.

He recalls the painful memory of his father disappearing into the distant trees, leaving him all alone. As for his mother, all he knows is that she is no longer in sight.

Feeling rather vulnerable from the voice's otherwise harmless question, the young boy feels embarrassed for not being able to hold onto his parent's devotion. His frail sense of worth had vanished for the simple reason that no one in world cared to claim him as their own.

"My mother and father left me without getting to know who I was," he explains, wondering again why he wasn't worth the effort.

Suddenly, his shoulders droop and eyes shut tight to hold back the tears that would only reflect his agonizing heartache. Any fear he may have felt suddenly left him as did his parents and identity before it.

He was no longer concerned for his whereabouts or worried about possibly dying as he realized that he had already lost everything that was dear to him.

At this point, he is entirely worn out from his pitiful condition and wishes only for his short, wretched life to end before he experiences any further sadness.

There was a long period of silence, as if someone was being mourned by the two nameless figures.

"I knew your father," utters the voice, breaking the uncomfortable silence, "not in person, but from a distance."

"What can you tell me about him?" asks the heartbroken child.

"He loved you very much," the anonymous voice tells him. "You could see it a mile away."

In the absolute sense, these were kind words

~ Who Are You? ~

from an invisible stranger. Yet they brought a deep sense of comfort to the visibly-wrecked youth. The boy manages to stop crying and sniffles in an attempt to regain his composure.

"Then why did he leave me?" he asks timidly, wanting desperately to know the reason.

"My dear child," the voice continues. "You are an exceptionally fine spirit and were only forsaken to keep from sharing in his misery."

The boy's eyes flutter as he struggles to open them. He straightens his shoulders and feels a renewed sense of being, realizing he was loved by his parents and worthy of their affection.

"You called me 'My dear child'. Do you intend to look after me?" the boy asks, expressing his lingering needs from being an infant.

There is a brief pause followed by the voice's gentle response.

"I spared you from the cold, lifted you from the forest, and fed you of my breast plate," the voice replies. "For me, we are already bound as mother and child."

~ My Dragon Mother: The Dragon's Cup ~

The young boy nods, acknowledging the voice's acts, further adding to the sincerity already present in its tone.

"If you would bind yourself in turn," the assuring voice continues. "Then yes, I would love and look after you for all time."

The child sighs; feeling redeemed once more by the voice's charitable proposal. Without hesitation, he states "You saved my life and gave me another."

It wasn't until then that he truly appreciated the magnitude of the anonymous spirit's benevolent gift. He pauses momentarily to keep from becoming overwhelmed, taking this time to clear his throat.

"It is not I who accept your generous offer," he continues, "but rather I who humbly seek to be called your son."

The boy then looks up towards the ceiling and exclaims "Please, let me look upon your gentle face!"

At once, the ceiling shakes and opens to reveal the full wing that had previously been wrapped around him in the form of a cavern.

~ Who Are You? ~

The young boy squints from the brightness of the sun and is temporarily blinded until he adjusts his vision.

He then stares in wonder as he witnesses a mighty dragon appear within his sight; as tall as the eldest trees and strong as the winds that break them.

His eyes glisten as the soaring dragon's iridescent scales shine in a wide array of colors, ever-changing with its slightest gesture.

The boy is awestruck that such an impressive creature would choose him above all others to share its life. His heart pounds with excitement as he searches for a way to embrace his newfound protector.

As the child steps forward, he notices the broken claw used to feed him and strokes it in a nurturing manner.

"How is this possible?" he asks.

"You have drunk of my milk and are no longer a mere mortal," conveys the shimmering dragon. "In sharing my life's force, you have already gained wisdom and talents beyond your years."

~ My Dragon Mother: The Dragon's Cup ~

The boy nods in acknowledgement and continues to listen closely.

"My milk will provide you with nourishment until you can draw life directly from nature's pulse, as I do."

The dragon then draws a string through the broken claw tip and places it as a necklace around the boy's shoulders.

"Until then," it instructs the child "you must keep this token with you and feed before the setting of the full moon. Otherwise, you will surely perish as do the leaves in the autumn sky."

The dragon continues to explain that with each feeding, the young boy will age at a much faster pace than his human brethren, which explains why he is able to sit, stand, and speak as he does this morning.

Lastly, on the night of the Blue Moon, the boy will complete the transformation and join his fellow magical beings as an immortal that no longer requires feeding via either plant or beast.

Thereafter, he will age slowly compared to his

~ Who Are You? ~

human companions so that he may seek and share knowledge over the span of many of their generations.

As a full wizard, he will be at one with all living things and may only fall through wounds received in battle.

The dragon then stood in silence to gauge whether the child was ready to embark on the path that it had laid before him.

"Are you ready then," she asks patiently, "to bind forever more as mother and child?"

With his arms outstretched, the young boy nods in acceptance for the role the benevolent dragon had bestowed -- though not fully understanding what such a life would mean.

Then with a resounding roar that shook the ground upon which he stood, the dragon looks to the heavens and proclaims, "I am Leona, Keeper of the Shifting Light. From today forward, I shall be known as mother to this human child. What is mine is also his. None shall dare harm him, for they shall face my ferocious wrath."

~ My Dragon Mother: The Dragon's Cup ~

The young boy's lungs filled with a warm sense of elation, seeing how openly she claimed him for all to hear. He knew of no inherent value that he possessed and wondered how he could be worthy of such an extraordinary honor.

His excitement, however, is quickly replaced by apprehension as Leona refocuses her pensive gaze upon him and circles his puny frame . . . like a serpent coiling methodically around its intended prey.

"Hmm . . ." she grumbles, sending a shiver down the boy's spine. "What should we call you, my young cub?"

He doesn't answer. It is clear from her tone that she is merely thinking aloud as she examines him in great detail.

Her question, however, is not one to be taken lightly. Having survived through the millennia, she is well aware of the power of a name -- how it could be used to describe or even define its bearer.

"What kind of wizard will you be?" she asks rhetorically, staring intently at the child as if peering directly into his soul.

~ Who Are You? ~

After all, he was not the first child to be transformed into a wizard. Over the years, Leona had come to know several human 'nieces and nephews' who were blessed with the power of magic.

Each of them was born through an act of kindness, though not all proved to be as compassionate as their immortal benefactors.

"Will you be a dark lord, ruthless and self-serving or will you be an enlightened guide and mentor, one to help the tribe of men climb from its vulgar state?"

The child looks away, fidgeting in a state of confusion. He wonders how he could possibly determine his life's journey at such a young age, even with the dragon's milk coursing through his veins.

Not wanting to displease his new guardian, he softly responds, "I will be . . . whatever you ask of me, my dear mother."

Leona praises the boy's loyalty and humility with a gentle tap on the shoulder and a thunderous burst of laughter. She then surrounds him even closer to ensure he feels her presence.

~ My Dragon Mother: The Dragon's Cup ~

"You will be . . . whatever you choose to be, my beloved," she declares with a grin. "I only hope to guide you so that your actions don't end in regret."

"I won't let you down," mutters the little boy with a slight nod.

Leona smiles and reflects on the sincerity of his words. She then declares, "I know what we shall call you, my darling son."

The little boy can barely contain his emotions knowing he will soon have a name of his own.

She leans forward and whispers in a soft tone "Emmerich" so that he would truly be the first to hear his name spoken aloud.

Feeling elated at finally having a sense of self, the young boy stands upright and repeats "Emmerich" softly to himself, relishing the sound of his name.

He then takes a deep breath and yells, "My name is Emmerich!" in his own childish roar, as if announcing his presence to the entire world.

Elated, the boy wraps his arms around the

~ Who Are You? ~

dragon's neck, smiling with his newfound identity, and softly kisses his mother's cheek.

Facing each other, they close their eyes in recognition of their special moment and say "I love you" in near unison.

~ My Dragon Mother: The Dragon's Cup ~

Chapter III

A Family, A Home

"Let's play a game!" shouts Emmerich. With his new height and speed, he couldn't wait to see what he could do.

"Very well, my child," replies Leona. "How about we play a game of 'hide and seek'?"

Perplexed, the young boy looks at his mother and asks "Where would you hide? With your enormous size, I could easily find you."

~ A Family, A Home ~

Leona grinned, thinking how young children, no matter their kind, really do have a gift for stating the obvious.

"Then, I shall attempt to find you, my perceptive cub," she replies.

"Okay, but your eyes can see farther than I could possibly run. How can I realistically hide from you?" inquired Emmerich with a hint of grouchiness ringing in his voice.

"Not to worry, my dear boy," she assures him. "I will teach you a trick to level our advantage."

Leona raises her head high into the air to look about the clearing. She spies a group of flowering bushes at the far end and asks, "Would you care to race?"

Emmerich gauges the size of her legs, trying to muster the will and energy for an extraordinary chase. Then he recalls the wing in which he was nestled the prior evening and slouches in unavoidable defeat.

"There's no way I could beat you. You are stronger than me in every way PLUS you can fly!"

~ My Dragon Mother: The Dragon's Cup ~

"Yes, you would be unsuccessful," his mother tells him. "Not for the reasons you observed, but because you have yielded solely to the apparent and failed to recognize what is already inside of you."

Leona proceeds to tell her son of how being a mystical being has many advantages beyond the gift of longevity. One of these talents is the ability to travel long distances within a short period of time.

"Some are blessed with the power of flight, as I am," she says flapping her wings slightly.

Emmerich's eyes widen with excitement as he immediately looks down towards his body, lifting his arms above his head in hopes of spotting his own set of budding wings.

There is nothing to show her. Emmerich turns to face his mother once more, slowly shaking his head in disappointment.

"Others," she continues, "can travel even faster by doing what I am about to show you."

"Are you ready?" she asks.

"Yes!" he exclaims, standing upright once

~ A Family, A Home ~

again.

Leona instructs the young Emmerich to see the bushes clearly, close his eyes, and recreate them in his mind.

"Do you see them?" she asks her son.

"Yes, but how is this . . ."

"Patience, my young cub," Leona interrupts. "Can you imagine yourself already there?"

"Yes, mother I can." he says in a calm tone.

"Then, open your eyes," she tells him, "and pick the flower on the branch to your right."

"Branch to my right?" asks Emmerich with his eyes still shut. "Your tail is to my right and the nearest flower is way over there on those far off bushes."

"Open your eyes, Emmerich!" yells Leona from a far off distance.

As Emmerich opens his eyes, he notices the change in his surroundings. He was indeed standing next to the vibrant bushes his mother had indicated.

~ My Dragon Mother: The Dragon's Cup ~

Suddenly, he vanishes from sight and quickly reappears under his mother's right wing.

"I have a present for you!" shouts Emmerich, handing his mother a yellow flower in an overt display of delight and accomplishment.

Leona smiles as she gently caresses her first gift as a mother. Though otherwise a common bud, this tiny symbol of his affection appeared to her as the most beautiful flower that had ever seen the light of day. She tucks it behind her right ear and poses for her young child to admire.

"You are a fast learner, young wizard," she says with pride in her son's abilities and kind nature, "Now, let's see how well you fare in a game of 'hide and seek'!"

Emmerich's mouth opens in awe as Leona swiftly pounces in his direction. She lands with a loud thump, releasing a gush of air that rushes out towards the trees.

She instantly checks beneath her torso, but the boy is nowhere to be seen. Instantly, he reappears atop her crown -- citing victory with his

~ A Family, A Home ~

narrow escape.

They play for hours, with Emmerich teleporting from one place to another . . . always leaving before his mother could find him.

Then it happened . . .

Emmerich elects to explore a point beyond the immediate tree line. Before long, he arrives at a section of scorched forest, giving a new meaning to the term 'black'.

Stunned, he stares at the remnants of the once-towering evergreens. His eyes catch glimpses of countless animal habitats, some with their seared inhabitants still trapped inside of them.

Emmerich feels the pain of the land as if it were his own, closing his eyes while mourning the incredible loss of innocent life. He hears their cries echoing through his head as they recount the tales of their gruesome passing.

Leona arrives shortly thereafter, finding Emmerich shivering in a hobbled state. She embraces her young son in an attempt to console him through this dreadful vision.

~ My Dragon Mother: The Dragon's Cup ~

"Let's see what happened." she says, making her way towards a fallen raven.

"Erat Spiritus Vitae," she whispers in a breathy tone.

Upon completing the incantation, a clear mist rises from around Leona's jaws. It comes together into a loose orb and then shifts into the shape of a winged dragon, reminiscent of her own powerful image.

The mist turns towards Leona, nods, and then flees swiftly towards the motionless corpse lying on the ground beneath her.

The mist wraps itself around the bird's crippled body until it is no longer visible, having been fully absorbed by the new host.

The dead bird stirs slowly at first, shifting the loose soil beneath. It then proceeds to twitch violently until its eyes are fully open, signaling that it is completely awake.

"How did this come to pass?" asks Leona.

The twitching slows, allowing the bird to

~ A Family, A Home ~

stand and face the mighty dragon who summoned it. The raven looks down towards its ailing body, trying to make sense of what is happening. It feels the unmistakably supernatural event in which it is now participating and answers his master's question.

"There were soldiers," it explains, gasping for a short burst of air into his crackling lungs.

Leona leans in closer, bringing Emmerich with her as they listen attentively to their obligated witness. The burnt raven's mind and body are clearly in excruciating pain, yet it continues to speak in the hopes of being released unto death once more.

"They burned a nearby farm, killing the humans who lived there," it testifies. "The fire then spread to the forest, killing the rest of us."

"What did they look like?" asked the dragon, hoping to narrow the list of suspects.

"They were large, heavy men encased in leather armor. They held a mix of sharp weapons, including swords and spears with the letter 'M' prominently inscribed in each."

With that, the raven collapses, releasing the

~ My Dragon Mother: The Dragon's Cup ~

borrowed mist from its decrepit torso.

Leona inhales deeply, luring the lent life force back to her being so that it may reunite with the breath already inside her.

She then falls forward, catching herself with her front claws. Worried, Emmerich rushes towards her and asks what he could do to help.

"That has never happened before," she mutters with a furrowed brow, indicating her concern.

"What was that?!?" asked the astonished boy. "How are you able to raise the dead?"

Regaining her strength, Leona replies, "It is called the 'Breath of Life' and apparently I can only share it for a short while."

She shakes her head as she thinks about how she had performed this feat many times prior and for much longer periods without any adverse effect.

"By speaking an ancient phrase," she explains, "I am able to connect with my spirit and channel its will."

~ A Family, A Home ~

Emmerich nods, wondering whether he would get learn such terms.

"With this specific incantation," she continues, "I am able to split my life's force and share it with whomever I please. In doing so, my own life is weakened until I regain what was initially lent."

The young boy and his mother sit silently as they reflect upon their own degree of sharing and its consequences, with one being the beneficiary and the other clearly the benefactor.

"Is it the same with me?" asks Emmerich with a hint of hesitation ". . . with the milk?"

"Yes," she replies, "all that is mine is also yours, including my life's force."

"I don't want you to die!" he exclaims, reaching his arms up towards her shoulders.

"Don't worry," she says in an uneasy attempt to comfort him. "Enough remains to sustain me until you are fully grown."

Feeling reassured, Emmerich lets out a sigh of

~ My Dragon Mother: The Dragon's Cup ~

relief. They smile nervously at each other as it appears nothing in this world is free, even in the realm of magic.

Looking about her, Leona decides to seek out a more secure setting. In doing so, she recalls the time when men were first encountered and how they were initially perceived.

Long ago, every tribal leader, representing all of the world's creatures, was called to an assembly of great importance. They came from every corner of the world; from the land to the sea and from the tropics to the arctics.

Not a single one of them was about to miss this historic event as they were about to meet their new chieftain.

It was a long anticipated moment and there was much apprehension about who would be selected. They had been promised a great and just ruler, one that would put an end to the incessant aggression and posturing that had been set in motion since the very beginning of time.

"What traits will dominate the new world:

~ A Family, A Home ~

claws, fangs, wings, or sheer size?" they debated amongst themselves.

It could be any one of them, though the dragons rose early as the speculative favorites. In a short while, they would come to know who was truly worthy of ruling over the rest.

At last, the wait was over and the first man was introduced in the global forum, resulting in shock and incredulity among many. Practically everyone sneered "THIS is the greatest being in all creation?!?"

The beasts, both eternal and mortal, arrogantly displayed the magnificence of their own characteristics to the solitary figure.

"Can you do this?!?" the animals taunted in a public comparison of abilities, much to the laughter of others.

"No," was his repeated answer. "You are better at it then I am."

Some of the more powerful beings scoffed and turned away from the absurd spectacle, seeing any comparison to be beneath them. They simply

~ My Dragon Mother: The Dragon's Cup ~

jibed at how this muddy figurine possessed only the feeblest of bodies; no claws, poor sight, blunt teeth, and a laughable amount of muscular strength!

It was Leona, standing silently among the heckling, who initially recognized his true gift. She slowly approached the confident man and peered into his body, seeing he had both the heart and mind of a god. The alpha female then bowed out of respect and welcomed him to his new land.

She was immediately met with a blast of ridicule and loathing by her peers for having sunk so low and so quickly.

"An alpha bowing to a worm!" they scoffed.

She shared with them what she saw and foretold how this race would one day rule the entire world.

"It is our duty to guide and protect them," she insisted, "for they will treat us exactly as they were once treated."

There was bitter disagreement among the beasts as they each saw themselves suddenly supplanted by the weakest among them. In a world

~ A Family, A Home ~

dominated by strength, they saw no reason to allow this feeble creature the necessary time to mature into their master.

In the end, the race of men was released into the world and a battle for dominion has raged ever since. Yet, for all the trouble that men have caused since their arrival, Leona felt pity for them and hoped they would someday realize their ultimate state.

Sadly, that day has not yet come. The human race is very young and still has the temperament of a feral child, seeking only what it wants without considering its impact on others.

"We must leave and go somewhere safe," she says in a somber tone. "We've seen what these soldiers can do and there is no telling what they are further capable of."

Just then, a twig snaps and both Leona and Emmerich quickly turn to face their transgressor.

"Perhaps I could help . . . with the 'somewhere safe' part of the conversation," squeaks a muffled voice from a nearby shrub.

"Show yourself!" bellows an emboldened

~ My Dragon Mother: The Dragon's Cup ~

Emmerich, with his powerful mother standing directly behind him.

The shrub begins to shake frantically in every direction with some branches bending to where they eventually snap.

After the miniature struggle comes to an end, the front branches finally part, giving way to a pair of tiny hands. They firmly grab a bunch of leaves and spread apart the conquered bush, revealing a young gnome as it steps forward into the clearing.

He was definitely young, even by gnome standards. It was clear just by his appearance that he had only recently left his parent's home.

The young gnome stood just below the average knee and had yet to produce a single whisker on his barely visible chin. As for his reddish hair, it was neatly combed and tucked under a drooped, but still somewhat pointed blue hat.

He wore brown leather boots with missing soles and donned generously oversized, spring-colored clothes -- likely so he could grow into them.

"Hmm!" he exhales loudly, looking behind

~ A Family, A Home ~

him as if the shrub still had some fight left in it.

"My name is Herman," he declares proudly, "and I am in search of a home and family to look after."

He then waits, almost as if to be congratulated for delivering his introduction exactly as it had been rehearsed; over, and over, and over again.

"We don't really have a home," explains Emmerich as he gazes up towards Leona. "We live wherever my mother takes us, right?"

Herman does not appreciate the odd objection and glares at the young boy in an attempt to quiet him, at least until he has finished making his presentation.

"Like I was saying," says Herman, focusing his attention on the decision-making dragon. "May I please have your name?"

"Leona," she replies with a smile.

"Luminous Leona, I come from a long line of attentive guardians, unmatched in the ways of defending a home," he claims proudly.

~ My Dragon Mother: The Dragon's Cup ~

Leona nods, acknowledging the accuracy of his words.

Emboldened, Herman continues to profess in a confident tone, "Nothing has ever gotten past any of my ancestors, and nothing will ever get past me!"

Recognizing his elevated tone, the young gnome simmers down and offers with a theatrical bow, "It would be my honor to protect your lair."

As odd as it appeared to Emmerich, the gnome's immodest offer was actually genuine. Time and again, this race of miniature soldiers had proven formidable in defending against a variety of malicious fiends. In the matters of security, there were few real alternatives to a vigilant gnome.

As for Herman, he was a particularly determined fellow who left home early in search of a grand adventure. He sought desperately to step beyond the accomplishments of his elders; a family tradition that ensured their honor would remain intact. If Herman would be permitted to guard a mighty dragon's lair, then he would undoubtedly have achieved his ambitious aim.

~ A Family, A Home ~

Leona smiles gently at the young gnome as he continues his chatty sales pitch and wonders if perhaps her son would benefit from the security and added bonus of a young playmate.

". . . I can navigate with the stars; I don't eat all that much; and my favorite color is . . . "

"We . . . ," the dragon interjects, "graciously accept your offer, young gnome."

Herman beams with excitement. He had passed on so many other, albeit lesser, opportunities in the hope that a truly great one would present itself. At last, it appeared that being selective and patient was indeed worth the wait.

"But be warned," she continues, "Guarding a young wizard is a challenge like no other, even for a brave race of guardians like the gnomes. Protecting my son, Emmerich, could very well lead to the loss of your own life."

Leona pauses briefly to gauge the young gnome's body language and concludes, "Are you willing to accept such a terrible risk?"

"A wizard AND a dragon?!?" shouts Herman,

opening his arms widely as if to express the enormity of the event.

"Whoa!!!" he exclaims, running his fingers rapidly through his freshly ruffled hair.

"This is WAY better than I could have imagined!" he shouts breathlessly as Emmerich and Leona look on, patiently expecting him to calm down at any moment.

"I mean, sure . . . my cousin Bertram guards a castle, a Baron's no less. But what is a castle, even a REALLY big one, when compared with guarding the pair of you?!?"

"Hmm", signals Leona with a clearing of her throat. "Your answer, if you please . . ."

"Agreed!" exhales Herman with a brilliant smile stretched across his face. "You won't be disappointed."

~ My Dragon Mother: The Dragon's Cup ~

Chapter IV

A Shield for a Sword

It is late in the day and the sun has just begun to set, casting long overlapping shadows in an already dark forest. Its creatures remain quiet within the safety of their sturdy nests as well-defined preparations are being made nearby.

"I can't wait to tell Bertram!" Herman mutters enthusiastically, as he paces in haste about the clearing. He had finally bound to a home -- a good home, and was cautiously preparing to secure the

~ My Dragon Mother: The Dragon's Cup ~

immediate perimeter from any intruders.

"How does this work?" asks an inquisitive Emmerich as he watches the gnome measuring the distance across several points.

Herman is preoccupied with the clearing of some debris and does not provide an answer.

"No offense," Emmerich continues, "but how could anyone expect for a tiny elf to protect such a powerful dragon?"

"ELF ?!?" Herman snaps impatiently, hoping to have heard incorrectly.

"When have you ever heard . . . of an elf . . . guarding . . . anything?!?" he asks with irritation in his voice.

Herman takes a deep breath in an attempt to calm himself before proceeding. He is not successful.

"I am a GNOME," he clarifies while waving his arms in the air. "We guard . . . we protect . . . to ensure nothing bad ever happens to our families."

"But, it's so dark out here and you're so . . .

~ A Shield for a Sword ~

small," blurts the boy.

"?!?" Herman stares in disbelief, "Did you hear the part about how NOTHING will ever get past ME?"

Emmerich nods that he remembers, but still has his doubts.

Herman sizes up the boy once more thinking that for someone his size, he really doesn't know much about anything.

"Watch . . ." signals Herman as he positions himself in an 'attention stance' and closes his eyes.

"Are you going to sleep?" asks Emmerich, waving his hand in front of Herman's face.

"No -- I am not going to sleep!" exclaims Herman. "It's just . . . well, this is my first time doing this, so just . . . give me some breathing space. Now, watch!"

Herman was right to be apprehensive. The feat that he is about to perform can only be realized by a bound gnome. It is not something that can be taught, but rather, only observed as a form of

~ My Dragon Mother: The Dragon's Cup ~

training.

The young gnome then checks the soles of his feet to make sure absolutely nothing is between him and the ground. He resumes his stance and this time, remains perfectly still.

He focuses on his breathing, adjusting the tempo as he searches for a precise, graceful rhythm. He inhales once more, holds his breath slightly . . . and upon exhaling . . . joins his heartbeat with nature's pulse.

"Bump, bum," echoes his heartbeat across the ground.

"Bump, bum" repeats the low-pitched boom as ghost-like waves emanate from just beneath his feet. They travel in every direction like ripples in a pond and can be seen flowing through the objects they pass before disappearing into the unknown.

At last, a figure emerges in the same hue as the peculiar waves that preceded it.

With an accomplished "Hello", Herman's smiling spirit addresses Emmerich directly.

~ A Shield for a Sword ~

The young boy is startled and jumps in surprise to see two like versions of his new companion standing next to each other.

"Are you dead?" he asks hesitantly of the specter.

"No! I am not . . . (gulp) dead," Herman insists with a smirk on his phantom face. "I am . . . everywhere!" he says, lifting his arms while twirling around in circles.

"How do you mean?" asks Emmerich, clearly not understanding the dizzying spirit.

Herman explains that while his tiny body remains in a sort of trance, his spirit if free to spread itself across the entirety of nature. To illustrate, he describes their seemingly silent scenery in precise, elaborate detail.

"Do you see those ants circling the moss-covered boulder?" signals Herman.

Emmerich nods.

"It's really their mound," he whispers, holding his hand to his cheek as if spilling a secret.

~ My Dragon Mother: The Dragon's Cup ~

"There are 3,609 of them patrolling the adjacent mound's exterior and 543,876 remaining inside," he states with his right index finger invisibly tracing the numbers in the mid evening air.

"Wow," exclaims an astonished Emmerich.

"Here, touch this tree," Herman continues. "It has exactly eleven climbable limbs with two more ready to sprout."

Emmerich pulls on a branch and starts to lift himself into the tree's crown.

"Not that branch!" yells Herman, reaching for the boy though unable to grasp him in his current translucent state.

"It looks strong, but it's not. I'll have to see about taking it down tomorrow so no one gets hurt," he says, making a mental note for himself.

Emmerich takes his friend's protective cue and cautiously returns once more to the safety of the ground beneath.

"Where was I?" Herman wonders aloud, "Oh yes, the tree! It boasts 8,624 flowers and 93,157

~ A Shield for a Sword ~

leaves, one of which just fell and landed right behind your left foot."

Emmerich was impressed with Herman's uncanny degree of perception. He had misjudged the gnome based on size alone -- never imagining the enormity of his vision.

"How far can you see?" he asks.

"I don't know," replies Herman. "I can connect with any living thing so long as it touches the ground."

"Is that why you don't wear shoes?"

"Of course I wear them, just not the soles. I have to touch the ground directly with my feet for the transference spell to work."

"Then why do you wear just the top half?" asks Emmerich.

"I need it to focus," Herman explains as he folds his hazy hands into a solid tranquil pose, "I have tried meditating barefoot, but just the thought of bugs crawling across my feet keeps me from being at peace -- you know, with nature."

~ My Dragon Mother: The Dragon's Cup ~

Emmerich laughs at the irony of Herman being so skittish when he is suppose to be in harmony with all living things.

Herman sees the humor in it as well and divulges "I don't know how they do it. Some of these elder gnomes stand guard barefoot and somehow can still focus enough to cover several villages at a single time."

The young boy is both impressed and confounded at how such a task could even be achieved.

"Who knows?" continues Herman, shaking his head. "Maybe someday, a really focused gnome will be able to see the entire world!"

They share an encouraging laugh. Who knew if it was even possible, but Emmerich decided that he would never underestimate his new friend ever again.

"That's odd," mutters Herman suddenly. "The trees are swaying without a passing gust of wind. It's as if they were being pushed down upon like . . ."

"A summer rain?!?" cries Emmerich.

~ A Shield for a Sword ~

"Yes!" agrees Herman. "Just like that . . . a summer rain!"

Emmerich was already familiar with the sensation of a downward wind. It couldn't have been his mother. She was clearly within his sight, resting calmly in the valley below after a long, exhausting day.

It was a dragon!

"We have to warn mother!" exclaims Emmerich as he teleports to Leona's side.

Herman returns to his body and looks on helplessly to see Emmerich reappear just as another dragon arrives on the scene. His eyes widen as he gauges the visitor's enormous mass and frightening appearance.

"What is it, my dear boy?" she asks Emmerich, not yet seeing the approaching creature.

"Mother!" he calls out. "We have company."

Leona looks up and instantly recognizes someone that she would rather keep at a distance.

"Vulferam!" cries Leona, frantically trying to

~ My Dragon Mother: The Dragon's Cup ~

hide her son.

The dark beast lands violently, hurling a vast amount of debris into the air with the power of an erupting volcano. He turns his jagged, stone-textured head and slowly covers Leona in a coil meant only to remind her of his immense size and status.

"Hello, my dear," he grumbles in a deep grinding tone. "Did you miss me?"

Leona shrugs her shoulders sharply to throw his rough, gravel-like torso off of her smooth, shimmering scales.

"What is this?" he grumbles inquisitively, spotting Emmerich as the young boy shuffles to reach the safety of her wing.

"Never mind him! What do you want?!?" she asks in an impatient tone, hoping to distract him away from her fragile son.

"Want?!?" growls the imposing beast, turning his attention back towards Leona, an exceptional prize apparently beyond his reach.

~ A Shield for a Sword ~

"You already know what I want, Leona. All I want is what's best for us . . . and our kind," he relays in a soft, compassionate tone.

In a firm voice, he adds, "To rebuild our ranks and not just settle for being part of this world, but to also be its masters."

This was an old argument that Leona did not want to revisit. She looks away in disgust, confirming once again that their views on the purpose and use of power were clearly at odds with each other.

Since they were young, Vulferam viewed strength as a divine indication of who should rule and who should be ruled. Being the most powerful among the immortals, he sought to impose a self-serving ideology where the strong dominate the weak.

Leona despised this belief system, recognizing other redeeming qualities like honor, courage, and compassion as being equally as important in defining the world's greatest leaders.

She advocated strongly for him and others to

see strength through a more benevolent light. She saw the gift of power as a means of maintaining life by protecting the more vulnerable among them.

In the end, Leona knew he would never change. She sees her might as a way to help others while he aims solely to enslave them.

"But for now," Vulferam continues in a more soothing demeanor, "I only want to hear how you've reconsidered my proposal. That you wish for us to bind so that you may provide me with the mightiest of offspring."

Sensing Emmerich's restlessness, Leona glances briefly between her enclosed wings and whispers, "Shh. Be still now. Everything will be fine soon."

"What is so important that you disregard the premier dragon of our time?!?" yells Vulferam as he pries open Leona's wings.

The alpha male's power is beyond belief, even to an immortal. In her weakened condition, Leona is simply unable able to oppose his overwhelming force.

~ A Shield for a Sword ~

With its cover removed, the empty space below reveals only Emmerich, an insignificant speck hurriedly adjusting his tattered rags in an attempt to look presentable.

Extending his hand in friendship, he states, "It is nice to meet y . . ."

"THIS is why you ignore me?" interrupts Vulferam with a shrill of disgust laced throughout his voice. "Then I shall remove your distraction so we may at last complete our union."

Vulferam turns towards the boy and conjures a massive swirling sphere of crackling purple flame. He hurls it directly at the unsuspecting child, covering him entirely in a private inferno.

Emmerich is stunned by the abruptness and intensity of the attack. He raises his arms in a feeble attempt to cover his face, as if doing so could really protect him from such a devastating assault.

Remarkably, he doesn't burn. Rather, he looks about him through the filter of violet rays circling in every direction. As they disappear, he surveys his body for signs of searing and pats down

~ My Dragon Mother: The Dragon's Cup ~

the residual blaze still flickering about his clothing.

"Don't tell me, Leona," sighs Vulferam disappointedly, his voice soaked in repulsion. "Don't tell me you have bound yourself to THIS."

Vulferam and Leona are the most powerful of all dragons and are commonly referred to as 'the alphas'. In the realm of magic, it is believed by many that the joining of their dominant bloodlines would form the mightiest of all creatures.

"Listen carefully, for I will not repeat myself," he says leaning heavily into her personal space.

Leona shrinks in an effort to shield her son from the encroaching menace; however, Vulferam interprets her apparently shy behavior as an act of submission and intrudes even further.

"You are mine," he declares. "And this . . ." he exclaims, motioning towards Emmerich "is an abomination."

The young boy shies away sheepishly, seeking the safety of his mother's folded wing once more. He had never before been referred to in such a contemptible manner and felt uncomfortable being

~ A Shield for a Sword ~

this close to his detractor.

Vulferam rises slightly so that he may look down upon the female dragon and proclaims "I will not tolerate such ludicrous behavior in this family!"

"Family? What family?" she retorts, "I never agreed to be yours in the first place!"

Visibly upset, the frustrated Vulferam sternly declares, "I have already bound myself; hence, don't have much of a choice . . . but then again, neither do you."

He then calls to Emmerich, "Come here boy! Be a good lad and let me squash you so that I may regain my destiny."

Having never before been threatened, the young frightened boy runs frantically towards the intimidating tree line. Though undeniably scared, he rushes desperately towards the dark forest's hostile embrace, knowing it to be the lesser of two evils.

Vulferam chases vigorously after him but is brutally tackled by the female alpha, allowing Emmerich to narrowly escape into the woods.

~ My Dragon Mother: The Dragon's Cup ~

"Go somewhere safe!" she yells at him through the interlocking gate of stalwart trees.

Nodding, Emmerich teleports to the safest place he knows . . . and reappears directly under his mother's wing.

Leona flings him away as she thrashes about with his aggressor. Emmerich continues to struggle with the security of his destination -- always appearing alongside his mother's wingtip, much to her dismay.

Finally, she turns towards her frightened child and instructs him to go far, far away.

"Go to the most beautiful place in the land," she says trying to mask her alarm as Vulferam delivers another crushing blow. "That way I will know where to find you when this is over."

Hearing the distress in his mother voice, Emmerich recalls how Herman was able to focus and promptly assumed his own 'attention stance'. He then summons all of his energy and focuses it into a single pressing goal, closing his eyes to hone in on such a splendid location.

~ A Shield for a Sword ~

Meanwhile Leona continues to endure Vulferam's vicious fists upon her back, each one a thunderous pledge for the survival of his lineage as wells as a thumping recompense for his unrequited affection.

As he crushes away at his intended, Vulferam thinks about how he could have chosen anyone for his bride. Yet, he picked Leona for the simple fact that she was the elite among the alpha females.

For him, their supreme positions of strength made them a perfect match. Nothing else mattered. The alpha male bound himself without hesitation, assuming she would do the same in recognition of his grand gesture.

He never considered how her unwavering stubbornness would result in the intense feelings of rage and lament he had come to know ever since that fateful day.

"The most beautiful place . . . the most beautiful place in the land," Emmerich repeats to himself until he ultimately disappears.

With her child free from harm, Leona's body

~ My Dragon Mother: The Dragon's Cup ~

finally yields and falls limp to the ground below. She is thoroughly exhausted, a dreadful feeling she had never experienced in her entire lifetime.

Vulferam pins his newfound victim forcibly to the floor, sensing her greatly diluted state. He is appalled by Leona's choice and subsequent weakness; feeling somehow cheated for having bound himself to someone so radiant on her exterior and so difficult within.

"I should kill you for your betrayal," he growls, "sharing your life with a worthless human!"

Leona turns away from him in disgust, though he continues to draw closer.

"I WILL have an heir and no lowly creature shall keep me from it. Enjoy your last day as a mother -- It will be over soon enough!" he threatens, launching swiftly into the midnight sky.

~ My Dragon Mother: The Dragon's Cup ~

Chapter V

The Search

Herman enters the clearing to glimpse Leona nursing her wounds, all the while calling out to her only child. She winces in pain with every movement; relaying the intense mental and physical suffering she feels across her flickering scales.

Leona can no longer sense her son and fears he may already be dead. With Vulferam on the hunt, she knows it is just a matter of time before Emmerich is found and broken.

~ My Dragon Mother: The Dragon's Cup ~

She senses Herman approaching, but continues to call with her unanswered wails echoing in the darkness. As the sound of her voice continues to dominate the landscape, she begins to tremble at the thought of Emmerich's continued absence.

Finally, Leona regains enough strength to fly and takes to the air, hoping to find her little boy before Vulferam ends him.

She continues her search across the land in vain, without a single sign of Emmerich's presence.

Having thoroughly examined the immediate patch of forest, the exhausted mother returns to see if Herman had fared any better.

As their eyes meet, they instantly know how unsuccessful their respective efforts had been.

Finally, Herman breaks the silence.

"I am sorry, Leona."

She offers neither rage nor comfort, just a disappointed sigh as she stares intently at the yellow flower Emmerich had given her earlier that day.

The loss of her child weighs heavily upon her

~ The Search ~

heart and she has absolutely no idea of how she is going to find him. She sits in silence and begins to ponder her next course of action.

Herman feels miserable at what had just happened. It was the first day of his new job and he had already lost the one person he was charged to protect.

He reflects on his boastful claims and realizes that had not yet earned the right to speak them. His arrogance led him to believe he was omnipresent; not realizing he had only connected to a small part of his environment.

The young gnome had learned a great lesson, but at an equally significant cost. In a single moment, Herman had somehow managed to disgrace his heritage, his trade, and himself.

"I just couldn't see him . . . flying through the air." he laments aloud, offering a hollow excuse for the lapse in their security.

Leona stretches out her wings and covers the gnome completely, to where nothing else is visible. Thinking himself doomed, Herman closes his eyes and braces for his well-deserved sentence.

Suddenly, he hears a loud crash that shakes throughout his being. He opens his eyes and is pleasantly surprised to see that it's not the crushing of his bones ringing through his ears.

A brief moment later, Herman hears another loud boom, and then a crash, just before it starts to pour down rain.

As the dirt floor dampens, Herman reflects on his last conversation with Emmerich. He smiles as he recalls how they laughed at the thought of being able to see the entire world at once.

'Heh . . . What a silly notion." he thinks to himself.

"But if it were indeed possible," he ponders "then surely, I would be able to find him!"

He explains the idea to Leona, who fervently shakes her head in disbelief.

"Not to be mean Herman," she says, trying to spare his feelings, "but you wear shoes during meditation to keep from being distracted."

~ The Search ~

Herman looks down at his feet, pressing his toes against the tops of his boots.

Leona continues, "No disrespect, young one, but how can you possibly expect to stay focused long enough to find my lost son?"

She was right. Herman knew that he had done nothing to earn her confidence. The land and possibilities were vast; Leona could literally spend years looking for the boy and never find him.

But her options were few and time was already running out on them. This young gnome was Leona's best chance of locating her son before either Vulferam or the full moon could hand him his fate.

"I can do it," he claims soberly. "I just need some help to pull it off."

'What do you need from me?" she prompts, indicating her agreement to proceed with his plan.

"I will need to be totally isolated in order to complete this task," he says, drawing an invisible sphere around his body.

"How do you mean, totally?"

~ My Dragon Mother: The Dragon's Cup ~

"If you could encase me in your wings, as before with the rain," he describes, "then I would know for certain that absolutely nothing will dare come near me."

"Okay," nods Leona, "I can do that."

"This would give me the calm I need to meditate deeply and find Emmerich," he assures her.

Herman realized the enormity of the task he had just promised to undertake. To his knowledge, such a thing had never been attempted, even by his barefoot elders.

Until today, the gnome's gift had been used solely to survey their immediate perimeter rather than to seek something beyond it. He was unsure as to how far he could project himself and if that distance would be sufficient to locate the missing child.

"I'm ready," Herman declares looking up towards the awaiting dragon.

Leona spreads her wings, allowing Herman to enter his water and bug proof abode.

The young, determined gnome summons all

~ The Search ~

of his will and courage as he looks for just the right spot beneath Leona's vigilant gaze. He then assumes his 'attention stance' between her wings and nods, instructing her to close them.

As his glimmering enclosure seals around him, Herman clears his mind and blocks any lingering doubts or concerns regarding his new quest.

He controls his breathing with an extreme degree of focus and successfully binds his heartbeat with nature's singular rhythm.

"Bump, bum" echoes the grey-blue pulse as it radiates away from the meditating figure. Herman's spirit leaves his body and reappears outside of the enclosure to address the visibly distraught mother.

"I don't know how long I can travel," he tells her, "but I shall not awaken until Emmerich has been found."

"Please hurry Herman," she pleads. "He hasn't much time."

"Fear not, Leona. I will find him," he promises with his eyes blazing, indicating his newfound level of focus and determination.

~ My Dragon Mother: The Dragon's Cup ~

Herman then sinks back into the ground and bursts outwards in every direction through ghost-like waves rippling across the forest floor. In an instant, he disappears entirely, leaving Leona to remain as his personal sentry.

The mother dragon is finally alone and exhales deeply, expressing her fatigue. She had just rescued Emmerich a few days once prior and once again, he is at risk of perishing -- or even worse.

Her mind starts to wander among the darkest possible scenarios involving her young son. She can't decide which is worse -- to starve or to be torn to pieces. In any case, neither would suffice as a suitable end for her dear, innocent child.

"No!" she screams in her mind. "Herman will find him."

Alas, she is hopeful but impotent. All she could do now is wait and stay vigilant to ensure the gnome's safety until he returns.

***

A full day passes without as much as a whisper from Herman. His body remains perfectly

~ The Search ~

still and Leona grows anxious for news of her son.

As the moon rises towards center, a lone wolf steps into the clearing on his way through the woods; walking slowly as he surveys the land, turning his head from side to side.

He is the scarred leader of his pack; with each healed wound visibly testifying to his cunning, strength, and continued dominance.

The wolf draws nearer towards Leona, awkwardly grinning as if to say 'Hello'. Not usually inclined to chat, he is clearly on the prowl.

"What a peculiar sight," he sneers, "a dragon guarding a gnome?"

"Keep moving, Rochus," she instructs with a stern tone. "This doesn't concern you."

"Leona, we are both creatures of the forest and thus tied to everything therein," he explains. "Any new development among the trees would surely concern the both of us."

Rochus had always been as crafty with his words as he had been with his actions. He had a terrible reputation for getting what he wanted by utterly confounding his unsuspecting victims. In fact, some regard engaging him verbally to be just as damaging as a physical confrontation.

"Have you lost something?" he pries, sniffing about in hopes of catching a whiff of something either dead or dying.

"How are Roma and the twins?" redirects Leona, knowing it was a sore topic for the heir-less alpha male.

On his exterior facade, Rochus appears to ignore her penetrating jab and continues inspecting the general area. But inside, he stirs at being reminded about the two human boys recently adopted by his intended mate.

Roma had found the infant children in the southern region while searching for food. Rather than killing the innocent babes as he would have, the she-wolf extended their dwindling lives by allowing them to suckle from her instead.

"Stubborn, as always," he insists, "still unwilling to provide a litter as long as those leaches

~ The Search ~

continue to linger in our den."

He keenly perceives Leona's worried expression and catches a faint scent in her vicinity. An innocent scent, one still untainted by the stench of temptation or deceit.

"(Sniff) . . . a child perhaps?" he poses, looking for nearby signs of its whereabouts.

The sly wolf continues deducing the identity of the mysterious guest with the few clues that remained. It is hard to discern since the rain had washed away most of the evidence.

Leona doesn't answer and continues to follow him with her suspicious eyes.

"You appear smaller Leona -- Perhaps not in size, but clearly in strength. Don't tell me you have decided to share your life's force with someone other than a dragon," he says with a sinister laugh.

Leona straightens her spine in an effort to appear taller and adjusts her wings to cover Herman a bit more securely.

"It's not the gnome. He is just the lookout."

he says dismissively beneath his breath.

"It must be (sniff) . . . a human?!?" he exclaims in utter surprise, "but that would drain you, isn't that right?"

Leona's expression indicates how she is taken back by his assertion of the child as well as of her physical demeanor.

"Oh dear me," he says mockingly with a huge smile he could barely contain, "what an ultimately futile endeavor."

"Spare me the lecture, Rochus," snaps Leona. "I heard it already!"

The wolf's eyes narrow as he lowers his stance into a more solid position.

"I am sorry old friend, but when the harvest suffers, so do the beasts that feed upon it . . . and those who feed upon them!"

He then releases a piercing howl and is joined right away by his hunting party. In the blink of an eye, Leona is surrounded by the most ruthless members of his pack.

~ The Search ~

One by one, the wolves mercilessly pounce on her in a daring attempt to feast upon fresh dragon meat, a prized delicacy for the rarity of its catch.

Leona is grounded due to her watching over the meditating gnome and screams with each grueling bite. She knows that if his feet lose touch with the floor, she would kill him along with any chance of finding her son.

She fends off a wolf at a time until their fierce coordinated effort begins to take its toll on her. As their battle rages into the early morning hours, the woods become filled with a myriad of snaps, growls, and the sound of shooting flame.

"I found him!" cries Herman, coming out of his trance.

The young gnome opens his eyes and is shocked at how different the scenery appears than when he left it. He looks down at his feet, reading the scrambled paw and claw marks across the wet floor, clearly illustrating the battle that must have just ended.

He smells the stench of burnt fur all around

him and sees bloodied wolves, either dead or running in the distance.

Having successfully fended off the wolf pack's attack, Leona crashes to the ground in complete exhaustion, having survived two inconceivable battles in such a short period of time.

While Herman remains unscathed through this ordeal, Leona's pale body is severely injured and lays motionless before the returning herald.

He climbs to be near her face and repeats softly, "I found him," as he proceeds to stroke her barely pulsing neck.

A long while passes before Leona's breathing finally steadies. Seeing signs of improvement, Herman regains hope and continues with his findings.

"Emmerich is safe, Leona," Herman reaffirms, "He is walking around a lake at the base of some mountains near a grand waterfall."

Leona sighs in relief, but cannot yet muster the will to acknowledge his encouraging message.

~ The Search ~

"It is a great distance, but I know where it is!"

The dragon's weary eyes open and Leona slowly stumbles to her feet, feeling the aches of a wicked double bludgeoning.

"If you know the way," she says with a renewed sense of purpose, "then I shall take us there."

Herman feels a rush of excitement knowing that the downtrodden dragon was back on the mend.

"Please let him know that we're coming," she kindly requests of him, "meanwhile, I will rest to recover my strength until you return."

Herman nods and quickly changes into his meditative state without any assistance. The single-minded gnome then rushes towards Emmerich as fast as he could possibly travel.

***

Half a day passes before Herman's spirit appears before the young boy, who is pointlessly searching for signs of a familiar setting.

"Look out for that root!" exclaims the gnome

as Emmerich walks in one direction while looking in another.

The young boy almost trips, again, but really can't be blamed for his distraction, given the recent series of distressing events.

"Don't worry, Emmerich," Herman assures, "now that I have found you, I can lead your mother to this location."

"What took you so long?" he asks, having pondered whether he had been abandoned once more.

"You are a long way from home," the gnome conveys somberly. "In fact, it will take us several days to reach you."

Emmerich sighs in disappointment as he receives instructions to take refuge in a nearby village and wait there until they arrive.

"One more thing, I almost forgot!" Herman exclaims, "Your mother told me to warn you to NOT use your powers or you'll risk draining your life's force! Quite frankly, I didn't even know you had any powers . . . until you simply disappeared

~ The Search ~

right in front of me when the other dragon showed up."

"Why?" Emmerich asks, "Why couldn't I just teleport back to her right now?"

"Emmerich, you don't have any control over where you end up. Teleporting somewhere else would only delay your next feeding," Herman explains. "And you know what that means," he says with a creepy expression indicating the child's demise.

The little boy nods, now fully understanding the spectrum of consequences.

"Lastly, I can't check in all that much as it will only slow us down in reaching you. Are you going to be okay on your own?" confirms the gnome.

"I'll manage," Emmerich says quietly looking away to control his emotions. "It's just that I already miss her and can't wait to be together again."

With that said, the young boy waves goodbye to his friend, allowing Herman to leave in order to begin his epic journey.

~ My Dragon Mother: The Dragon's Cup ~

With Herman's departure complete, Emmerich immediately starts walking in the direction the gnome had indicated. The young boy feels encouraged knowing his family would eventually be reunited -- how and when is anybody's guess.

As he surveys the foreign land, he pauses and inhales deeply to collect his strength . . . for once more, he is alone and frightened.

~ My Dragon Mother: The Dragon's Cup ~

Chapter VI

The New Boy

It is late afternoon when Emmerich finally stumbles into the lakeside town of Schön, ancient homestead of the Bavarii people and supposed location of the mythical Röthbach Falls.

It is a majestic setting, nestled at the base of Mount Watzmo, the highest peak in all the land. The lake's crystal waters enhance the premium view by effectively doubling the blend of green, blue, and white tones via its extra-wide reflection.

~ My Dragon Mother: The Dragon's Cup ~

Emmerich couldn't have found a more perfect setting to fit his mother's final set of instructions.

"Go to the most beautiful place in the land," he repeats softly to himself. "I definitely found it," he smiles proudly.

Acting on Herman's instructions, he approaches the main gate of the walled village and introduces himself to the first-year guard standing at its entrance.

At first, the thin guard with oversized armor ignores the approaching boy, assuming him to be a local youth in search of mischief.

Emmerich clears his throat.

"Hmm, excuse me sir. I am lost and far from . . ."

"You're not from around here, are you?" interrupts the guard, leaning in closer to see whether he recognizes the youth.

"No sir, I am lost and far from home. Please let me in so I that may have shelter." Emmerich asks

~ The New Boy ~

in his politest tone.

The guard looks him over and signals to his commander in the tower above.

"What is it?!?" he yells.

"This child is lost and not from around here," he explains. "What should I do with him?"

The commander climbs down and assesses the boy's condition for signs of disease, effectively training the new cadet for the next such occasion.

"He's clean," the commander declares. "Take him to the town center."

Emmerich is led through the winding streets of the walled village, where he promptly notices the vast disparity between Schön and his hometown.

"This appears to be a considerably more prosperous nation," he thinks to himself.

The young boy is astonished by the number of happy families walking among the town's homes and shops. There is much activity in the marketplace, the grounds are kept tidy, and even the humblest among them wears shoes.

~ My Dragon Mother: The Dragon's Cup ~

He looks down at his own attire and feels embarrassed. His burnt, soiled rags practically scream, "He is not from here! He is from a much lower place!"

Finally, he is brought before the town council, the local ruling authority that would ultimately decide what to do with him.

As he waits his turn to address them, Emmerich tries to think of a reason as to why the townsfolk wouldn't just throw him back into the wild. He doesn't want to be a burden on his hosts, but is also low on ideas on how to contribute meaningfully.

After a short period, the hunched self-conscious youth is called forward to state his request. As he steps past entire rows of torches, leather, and iron, Emmerich finds his hands nervously attempting to stretch out the wrinkles between the tears that highlight his ragged clothing.

Emmerich looks up towards a raised platform to gaze upon the seated council, a regal looking group who distinguished themselves from the common townsfolk through the liberal use of

~ The New Boy ~

precious metals in their arms and clothing. In addition, each wears a gold ring bearing the mark of an aggressive dragon, the heraldic symbol of their ancestors.

At its center sits Tancred, their chieftain. He is a tall dark majestic figure with an elaborately bejeweled sword adorning his hip. He is a Baron by birth, but yielded his supreme rule over the township long ago when collaboration appeared to be the only way to salvage their way of life.

To Tancred's right sits his bride, Mathildis. She is an astonishingly beautiful woman with eyes in the tone of water and long flowing hair the color of wheat. Her sharp wit and beguiling manners left no doubt as to whether she belonged in the ruling class.

Next to her is Raban, the high priest and spiritual leader of the realm, a short wiry man who speaks and giggles often to himself. Though he seems odd in his behavior and appearance, his counsel is sought on practically every subject, especially on those pertaining to the unknown or supernatural.

On the chieftain's left sits Othmar, a large and

~ My Dragon Mother: The Dragon's Cup ~

heavy blacksmith with metallurgical skills significantly beyond his peers. His talents were widely regarded, especially in the craft of advanced weaponry.

Lastly at the end sits Andreas, the brooding captain of the guard sworn to protect Schön's borders. His lineage is filled with conquerors and heroes whose acts still ring in local folklore. It is no secret how he yearns to join them in such a tradition.

Emmerich looks up to the council in hopes of being afforded a comfortable place to live -- just for a little while, until his mother comes for him by month's end.

"Where are your parents?" asks Tancred.

"I am alone," replies Emmerich. "I got lost in the forest and my mother is a long way off."

"She left you?" inquires Mathildis with an inquisitive grin, rising slightly in her chair to gauge his expression.

"No," replies Emmerich, looking down towards his feet. "We just got separated and now she is on her way to find me."

~ The New Boy ~

"Something is not right -- I can feel it." Andreas whispers to his cohorts. "This boy is not what he seems. Perhaps he is a scout for an invading army. You know there is much conflict to the West."

"He is a mere child!" scoffs Othmar loud enough for Emmerich to hear him. "Besides, what kind of threat can we expect from an army that depends on the likes of him?" he mocks, drawing the contrast in size with their own impressive stature.

"All the same," utters Raban, "we should keep him close and prevent any information from reaching his battalion."

They nod to each other in agreement.

"How old are you boy?" asks Tancred.

"Seven!" blurts Emmerich. It sounds like a good number.

"You are too young to labor in anything useful," Tancred declares, "hence; you will be placed in the care of the Waisenhaus until such a time that someone claims you or until you are able to contribute something to our society."

~ My Dragon Mother: The Dragon's Cup ~

Upon sealing the proclamation, Emmerich is escorted out of the judicial forum and is then taken to his new accommodation at the town's orphanage, the Waisenhaus.

By the time he arrives at his new home, it is dark and everyone has already gone to sleep.

***

The next morning, Emmerich is greeted by the sounds of screaming children playing in the courtyard located just outside his bedroom window.

He opens his eyes and is met by a short, stern-looking woman with her long black hair tied neatly into a bun. She is Roza, the school's administrator, and she had only been notified of the new youth's arrival a few moments prior.

"You got to sleep in because you arrived so late," she declares. "From now on, you will rise and set with the others."

Gesturing for him to get up, she notices the tattered rags that barely draped him. He had scrapes across his knees and was covered in dirt from head to toe.

~ The New Boy ~

Shaking her head, she leads him to the bath, mumbling, "It's hard to believe how savage children become when they are left unattended."

There, she scrubbed and scrubbed, and scrubbed again until her unfounded fears of lice were completely alleviated.

Many suds later, Emmerich is squeaky clean and is instructed to towel off behind the mirror. She hands him a white oversized shirt and a pair of grey trousers that fit in the waist, but don't quite reach down to his ankles. Shoes had to be made, so they would have to wait.

Roza calls Emmerich to view himself in the mirror. This is the first time he has seen his reflection and is pleasantly surprised by his appearance. He waves his arms, tugs at his hair, and counts the number of teeth; ending his assessment with a smile.

"From now on, this is how I expect you to look," Roza says firmly. "Do you understand?"

"Yes," Emmerich tells her, reinforcing his acceptance with a nod.

~ My Dragon Mother: The Dragon's Cup ~

"Off you go then," she tells him with a wave, feeling an immense sense of pride for his dramatic transformation.

***

Emmerich eagerly finds his way into the noisy courtyard, taking in the sight of so many happy children to play with.

"Where do I start?" he thinks to himself, never before having had such an abundance of choices.

Paralyzed in indecision, Emmerich is snapped out of his delightful trance by a petite girl in a white sundress running towards him with long wavy hair reminiscent of the sunflowers that grew near his childhood home.

"My name is Claudia. What's yours?" she asks, catching her breath slightly.

The young boy is pleasantly stunned by his hostess's charming demeanor and lapses in his reply.

"Uh . . . I am Emmerich," he says proudly, this being the first time he has ever introduced

~ The New Boy ~

himself.

"That's a stupid name!" calls another voice.

Emmerich turns around, but is unable to distinguish the person speaking through the frenzy of children screaming.

"Don't listen to Fulco," Claudia advises. "He's a jerk."

Just then, Emmerich is approached by a thin muscular boy in fine dark clothing and amber colored hair. With him are two other rosy-cheeked boys who appear to be among the oldest in the playground.

"What did you call me?" Fulco asks, pressing his shoulder into Emmerich's face.

"I didn't say anything," mutters Emmerich apprehensively, taking a slight step back to better see his young aggressor.

Fulco snickers at the new boy's harmless facade, gloating with his cronies as bullies tend to do.

"I am new here," Emmerich adds, offering his tiny hand in friendship.

~ My Dragon Mother: The Dragon's Cup ~

Fulco looks down his nose at the new boy's extended arm. He notices his apparently borrowed attire, confirming his initial suspicion. Fulco then slaps Emmerich's hand away and points to the decrepit building behind him.

"You're the new drain at the Waisenhaus, aren't you?" he sneers, looking towards his associates for a laugh at the new boy's expense.

"Isn't this all one place?" asks Emmerich, motioning his arms out towards the corners of the courtyard.

"Goodness, NO!" exclaims Fulco with his hand rubbing his right temple in disbelief.

"This courtyard is part of our school, the Kindergarten," he explains. "We let your kind play here so the pitiful can have something to aim for."

"What do you mean pitiful?" Emmerich asks feeling disrespected, taking a large step forward towards the offensive child.

"People like you," Fulco points out insensitively. "My father told me how you came here begging last night from out in the wild."

~ The New Boy ~

Emmerich is stunned and does not dispute his words. He did ask for assistance -- He just never expected it to be thrown back in his face.

"I would never do such a thing!" Fulco proclaims proudly. "If I want something, I work for it -- plain and simple. But how could I expect trash to possibly understand? All your kind knows how to do is to take from the fruits of good, hard-working people like us Bavarii."

Fulco's intolerable rant draws the attention of everyone in the courtyard, bringing all of its play and merriment to a sudden uncomfortable close.

"But these are orphans," explains Emmerich compassionately. "None of them chose to be here. They have already suffered more than you could ever imagine and aren't deserving of your hostility."

Unmoved, Fulco remains convinced of his nauseating position, reassured by others who silently felt exactly as he did.

"Don't bother, Emmerich." interrupts Claudia. "You can't reason with the unreasonable," she says, pulling him away from the 'unwelcoming

~ My Dragon Mother: The Dragon's Cup ~

committee'.

"Come on," she says. "Let's have some fun!"

~ My Dragon Mother: The Dragon's Cup ~

Chapter VII

Having Fun

Claudia introduces Emmerich to several other warm and hospitable children, completely disregarding whether they entered the courtyard through Kindergarten or Waisenhaus.

"What shall we play?" asks Emmerich full of anticipation.

The mass of children erupts at the chance of picking a game for all of them to play.

~ My Dragon Mother: The Dragon's Cup ~

"How about Fangen?" asks Odo.

"No, Topfschlagen!" yells Frida.

"Stopessen! Stopessen! Stopessen!" shouts Uschi, the smallest of the bunch.

"Stopessen?!?" asks Claudia looking down at the youngest among them, "How are we to play Stopessen with nothing to eat?" she asks with her hand placed sternly on her hip.

Uschi raises her hands and shakes her head without saying a word. Apparently "Stopessen" is one of the few in her vocabulary.

"How about Fangen?!?" yells Odo, finally victorious over the squeaky chatter.

No one declines.

"Tag, you're 'it' new boy!" he yells, slapping Emmerich eagerly on the shoulder before swiftly running away.

Suddenly the rest of the children start screaming "Run!!!" and proceed to frantically do so in every possible direction.

~ Having Fun ~

Emmerich doesn't understand, "I thought we were supposed to play a game!" he yells walking towards the dispersing crowd.

"You've never played Fangen?" asks Claudia, stopping in surprise that someone his age had never done so.

"What am I suppose to do?" he asks with a perplexed look on his face.

"Alright, but don't touch me," she insists, walking towards him with her hands in a guarded position, "I don't want to be 'it', at least not yet."

Emmerich nods and Claudia comes closer to teach him the rules of the activity.

"Odo called the game, so he gets to choose the first person to be 'it', that's you," she explains gesturing towards the new boy.

"Now, you need to catch one of us to make a new 'it', and so forth. Get it? Haaa, get 'it'?!?" she laughs, looking for a sign that he appreciates her sense of humor.

"Got 'it'!" laughs Emmerich as he starts to

run, sparing her, for now, because of her kind Fangen instruction.

The children run after each until each of them had a turn at being the chaser among the pack of fleeing victims.

"What next?" Emmerich asks, clearly not yet tired from all of the running.

Frida steps into the middle of the miniature crowd and drops a rusted helmet she found in the nearby bushes, watching it clang until it finally settles near the small circle's edge.

"We can play Topfschlagen," she suggests, looking for signs of approval. "It's not a pot, but it's metal. It's close enough, right?"

'I'll get the prize!" calls Claudia.

'I'll get the stick!" exclaims Leuthar. "Who wants to go first?"

The children rush to secure their ingredients and reassemble once more. A few minutes later, Claudia returns from hiding the prize under the helmet and rejoins the group.

~ Having Fun ~

"Since you're new," Claudia says facing Emmerich, "you get to go first."

Leuthar returns just after and hands a stick to Emmerich, who is clearly at a loss of what to do next. He simply holds it while shrugging his shoulders in hopes that someone will volunteer some information.

"Let me guess," Claudia says with her index finger tapping softly upon her twisted smile, "you've never played Topfschlagen either."

"Not yet," he replies.

"Alright, you're 'it' again, which means you get to close your eyes and tap the ground with your stick," she explains,

"Like this?" Emmerich asks.

"Yes, just like that. Meanwhile, we'll yell 'hot' or 'cold' which lets you know if you're getting closer. The game is over when you 'hit the pot' and claim the prize within."

"Let's do it," says Emmerich with his eyes completely shut.

~ My Dragon Mother: The Dragon's Cup ~

"Ready? No peeking!" yells Claudia.

"Set . . . Go!" the children shout, laughing aloud as the new boy struggles to find his target.

"Hotter!" yells one child.

"Colder!" yells another.

The screams continue until Emmerich becomes totally confused and loses track of his direction. Not wanting to give up, he continues shaking his stick as he recklessly traverses the ground beneath.

The children laugh and hurriedly jump out of his way, ensuring their feet don't get pummeled. Eventually, the young blind boy admits defeat, having crashed into a bush marking the start of a large field.

"That was funny," calls Claudia, smiling as she and the other children walk towards the fallen boy.

Leuthar and Odo help Emmerich climb out of the bushes, laughing as they recount the crazy path their new friend had just taken. They start telling tall tales and laugh at each other's jokes. Before long,

~ Having Fun ~

they lose track of time and eventually turn their attention towards the grumble in their bellies.

Claudia grips her side and says, "Too bad the harvest is over. This is the sweetest Heidelbeere field for miles."

Emmerich senses how hungry his new friends had become and decides to help them. He recalls Herman's warning about using his power, but figures it was only a few berries and there wouldn't be any real harm.

While the children continue playing, the young boy leans down towards the base of a nearby bush and politely asks if it would share some of its fruit with his hungry friends.

"I don't ask any for myself," he says humbly, "just enough so they don't go hungry this evening.'

The bush is touched by the child's kind gesture and acknowledges his request by shaking its leaves, though no gust of wind is otherwise felt. However, the growing season had already passed and the bush is simply unable to oblige Emmerich's request.

~ My Dragon Mother: The Dragon's Cup ~

"If only I had sufficient light," a soft voice tells him in his mind, "I would gladly give you my fruit."

Emmerich acknowledges the bush's words and thinks for a moment, but nothing comes to mind. Losing himself in thought, he gently nibbles on his right thumbnail.

"I got it!" he thinks to himself.

The young wizard looks to the sky and gauges the height of the late afternoon sun. He then takes off his necklace and centers his mother's claw over the bush that spoke to him.

"I'll channel the sunlight through my mother's funnel," he whispers, "I just hope it works the same as it does for milk."

Emmerich places the narrow end of the claw to his lips and inhales deeply to start a siphon. With his breath as a primer, the dragon's claw starts to draw down the sun's life-giving energy towards the awaiting Heidelbeere bush.

As it gains strength, the space above them slowly begins to swirl with a combination of wind

~ Having Fun ~

and light. The young boy continues to steadily hold the claw over the bush as it glows to a bright amber tone.

The swirling motion grows stronger with each revolution until it finally evolves into a miniature tornado, pulling the hovering clouds down towards the ground. The bright sky darkens as the clouds further condense and draw closer.

"I think it's going to rain!" yells Frida, climbing down from a distant tree.

Panicked, the young wizard pulls the glowing claw towards his chest. The siphoning continues and tugs at his hair, clothes . . . even his own life's force. Finally, in an act of desperation, he covers the funnel with his palm and watches in relief as the swirling wind dies down to a tranquil pace once more.

Emmerich drops to his knees and takes a moment to catch his breath. As he starts to rise, he sees the fruit of his labor -- a fresh batch of sweet Heidelbeeren sprouting at their peak of ripeness.

"Thank you," he whispers to his silent companion.

~ My Dragon Mother: The Dragon's Cup ~

Emmerich then turns and yells "Look over here!" as he displays a large, luscious Heidelbeere held between his thumb and forefinger.

"Talk about a late bloomer!" shouts Claudia as she and the other children lunge towards the awaiting bush.

They happily eat their fill and carry some of the juicy Heidelbeeren back towards the main area, staining both cloth and skin.

"Now we can play Stopessen!" yells Uschi as they approach the courtyard's center. The children laugh and say their farewells as they start making their way to their respective homes.

As the smiling children disperse, Fulco glares intently at the luscious batches of fruit and pinches Claudia's share.

"Hey -- That's mine!" she cries in dismay. Though usually feisty, she is considerably smaller and knows not to press for their return.

"Not anymore," Fulco smirks, savoring the spoils of his brute force.

~ Having Fun ~

Emmerich steps between them and pulls back Claudia's share of the fruit. A silence falls over the courtyard as the new boy's bold act will likely result in a beating.

"You know the way to the field," Emmerich grumbles in a low, serious tone. "Next time, pick them yourself," he says, handing the stolen fruit back to Claudia.

The two boys stare intensely at each other, neither one of them backing down from their confrontation.

Suddenly, there is a loud burst of laughter flowing from the awed spectators. The mere idea of Fulco picking anything was simply too shocking of an image for the crowd of children to bear.

Red-faced in anger, Fulco spits on the ground in front of Emmerich and storms away.

***

Later that night, as the orphans sleep in their beds . . . Fulco and his two thugs stealthily approach the Waisenhaus dormitory.

~ My Dragon Mother: The Dragon's Cup ~

"I'll show him," Fulco grumbles under his breath as they sneak unto the premises. "Come on. Let's put the soot back on his cheeks."

The two boys glance at each other and then stare at their sadistic leader, clearly second-guessing his violent intent.

"Are you just going to stand there or are you going to hand me that torch?" he says in a commanding tone.

"Isn't this going a bit too far?" questions Gunda while clearing his throat, "Calling someone names is one thing, but causing them permanent injury or even death is quite another."

Fulco gives Gunda a dirty look and forcibly snatches the torch from him, yanking his crony's hands in the process.

"Give me that since you obviously lack the courage," chides Fulco.

As Gunda rubs his hands gently to help them recover, Fulco rubs the torch furiously against the building to burn it.

~ Having Fun ~

"Some people just need to learn their place." he growls, feeling the torch's heat as he shakes it back and forth.

Suddenly, a flash of fire splashes along the side of the decrepit wooden frame. It reaches higher and higher and then spreads across the rooftop. Fulco's eyes beam with delight as the flames make their way down into the floor below, withering away at what he saw as an unnecessary eyesore.

The children awaken to the alarming sound of crackling timber. They open their eyes and see the roll of menacing fire hovering over their beds. Smoke fills the rooms below and forces a miniature stream of coughing figures to cascade through the side door.

"Where's Claudia?" asks Roza, taking a rapid inventory of the frightened children.

"Claudia . . . a Waisenhaus?!?" cries Fulco in disbelief. "I thought she was one of us."

While not exactly friends, Claudia is the one person with qualities that Fulco seems to admire. She consistently stands up to him, a rarity considering boys twice her size would rather run than face his wrath. In his mind, this little girl exemplifies the true Bavarii spirit with her delicate blend of strength and beauty.

Without hesitating, Fulco races into the burning building in search of his one worthy opponent. He couldn't let her perish -- Not her, not through his action, and definitely not like this.

Before long, the heavy smoke overwhelms him and he loses consciousness in the center of the main sleeping area.

The fire rages and none dare enter the orphanage for fear of losing their own life. Within minutes, help arrives from the village with teams of men and women splashing buckets of water, hoping to contain the roaring flames.

Suddenly a small figure emerges from the smoldering edifice, dragging two still bodies behind him. It's Emmerich!

With a handful of clothing in each fist, he drags Fulco and Claudia by their collars, breathing deeply with each determined tug. As he exits the

~ Having Fun ~

crashing building, two adults relieve the young hero and carry the unconscious children to a blaze-free zone far from the falling embers.

Emmerich follows them to their resting place and repeatedly shoves the two children to get them to awaken, but does not get a favorable response. With the adults clearly pre-occupied with the roaring inferno, he leans down and speaks, "Erat Spiritus Vitae" in the same breathy tone as his mother did several days prior.

A small spray of transparent mist emanates from his lips and settles into the shape of two young boys. They walk out into the midnight air, gazing up at the young wizard and then look briefly towards each other.

Suddenly, the two phantoms smile and signal each other with their ghostly fingers "1-2-3" before racing towards their respective targets. Upon reaching them, the small boys quickly dissolve and become absorbed into the still bodies of their new hosts.

Within seconds, Fulco and Claudia awaken in a haze from their smoke-induced slumber, feeling fortunate to have delayed their final end. The lent breath then leaves their bodies without their knowledge and returns once more to its awaiting master.

Meanwhile Emmerich drops to his knees. Though neither child had died, his act of revival left him feeling tired and week.

Just then, Tancred and Mathildis of the council arrive and immediately head towards their son's unexpected savior.

"Thank you for rescuing our son," says Tancred, gently brushing Emmerich's shoulder before making his way back towards his wife and child.

Emmerich looks on as Fulco is hugged and kissed by both of his parents, a feeling he does not remember for himself.

As the young wizard catches his breath, he dwells on the fresh image of a perfect family and begins to wonder why he has been cursed with such rampant misfortune.

For regardless of his appearance, Emmerich is

~ Having Fun ~

still very young and has had little time to either inspire or offend anyone.

The young boy struggles to comprehend his situation. From his perspective, he has never intentionally caused harm yet has already lost his parents twice.

Meanwhile, Fulco didn't appear to know what 'being nice' meant and was incredibly blessed with a loving family.

~ My Dragon Mother: The Dragon's Cup ~

Chapter VIII

A Celebration

The following day, the village council convenes bright and early with a significant mass of it constituents to account for the previous night's events.

"What happened last night is a tragedy," proclaims Tancred. "These children have lost their home and the cold months are quickly approaching. With your help, we will rebuild the Waisenhaus in time for their salvation."

~ A Celebration ~

The silence that follows is awkward for everyone as the chieftain had anticipated a round of applause indicating their support. Instead, his comments are received with suspicion and resentment as his deflection of responsibility felt too much like the old days when the Barons ruled with impunity.

"How could he stand there and claim leadership when one of his own is to blame for this disaster?" the villagers think to themselves.

There is a restless stir among the crowd. Though many of the villagers had come to rebuild the new orphanage, many more had assembled to get closure on what had occurred the night before.

"What about the arson?!?" yells one of the frustrated villagers.

Tancred looks silently down towards his feet in an attempt to calm himself, though rages internally for the shaming of his family name.

Fulco had always been arrogant towards his classmates, but it was traditionally expected since he was genuinely of noble birth. However, since the council was formed, the villagers had become increasingly intolerant of such behavior.

"This would never have happened before," Tancred thinks to himself. He felt disgraced for having to account for anything, much less publically for the actions of his juvenile son.

After a brief pause, Tancred turns and glares at Fulco, who is standing quietly behind him on the left. The young boy takes a few timid steps forward and is pushed to the front by his disappointed father.

Fulco stands alone before the irritated crowd and publically apologizes for his reckless act of vandalism.

"I . . . I didn't mean for this to happen," he states nervously, feeling the intensity of the town's collective glare. "I only wanted to scare someone and I am truly sorry."

Fulco's display inspired the same feeling in which it was uttered. His words came across as being cold and disingenuous, but it was a public apology all the same.

Before anyone had the chance to speak their

~ A Celebration ~

mind, Tancred immediately steps in front of Fulco and positions his son out of the public's direct view.

"As the boy's father, I can assure you that he has been appropriately reprimanded," he says, abruptly shifting topics. "Now, let's get to the business at hand and provide these orphans with a new home."

"That's it?!?" several of the villagers mumble.

"Someone could have died!" one calls from a distance.

The townsfolk were clearly unsettled and wanted more than simple words to make things right. Fulco steps back from the overwhelming contempt of his father and the restless crowd. Sensing the villager's simmering need for justice, Tancred offers an acceptable distraction to redirect their will.

"As a token of our family's appreciation, I will personally sponsor a festival in honor of the rebuilding effort."

The villager's ears perk up when the festival is mentioned as one was not due until the fall. None dared object to this grand gesture, especially if was to be done on their behalf.

"I shall provide food, drink, and entertainment upon completion of our task," he promises. "So, the sooner we get going, the sooner we can commence with the festivities. Now, who's ready to get started?"

The crowd roars in excitement and immediately begins to tear down the charred remains of the old dormitory. They hum and sing traditional Bavarii tunes as they work towards the social reward that awaits them.

After a full day's work, the villagers had managed to build a base shelter for the few among them who did not have a home. It wasn't the grandest of buildings, but neither was it expected to be. After all, how would it look if the dwelling of an orphan surpassed the home of an intact family?

***

Good news travels quickly in the Bavarii valley, especially when a celebration is involved. With the evening soon approaching, the villagers begin to gather in the town's center, bringing with

~ A Celebration ~

them all sorts of aromatic treats; including braided strudel, wurst, and bier.

Emmerich and Claudia arrive early and start to roam the festival grounds.

"Thanks for saving my life," says Claudia while holding her rescuer's hand.

"You're my friend," he replies. "I'm sure you would have done the same for me."

"They didn't mention you when the festival was announced," she informs him as she shakes her head in disbelief, "making it instead a tribute for the new building."

"That's alright," Emmerich replies. "I didn't do it for the recognition."

"All the same," she continues. "I wouldn't be here if it wasn't for you . . . so in my mind, this festival is for you as well as the others."

"Come on," says Emmerich, pulling Claudia by the hand. "Let's see what they have set up for us."

As the sun fades in transition to the evening

night, the village begins to fill with travelers and hunters who have come to trade their goods -- mainly for the bier.

They bring kirschwasser from the far western lands and tell tales of a fearsome dragon circling in the night sky, devastating entire villages along the way. Many speculations are conjured as to why -- the most popular being that someone had stolen its egg.

"It couldn't be my mother," Emmerich thinks to himself. "She is kind and values the preservation of life, plus she knows exactly where I am through the aid of Herman's spirit."

It had to be Vulferam! Who else would be so brutal in searching through an unsuspecting village? It appears that he had not given up his quest to be rid of the young wizard after all.

Emmerich shivers as he remembers the look of disdain the alpha dragon had given him. The young boy knows it was just a matter of time before they would meet again. He just hopes his mother is able to find him before his would-be-slayer.

Claudia snaps Emmerich from his dismal

~ A Celebration ~

thoughts by showing him all of the wonderful attractions that had been assembled for the evening. It is a cheerful atmosphere with lots of music and revelry. In addition to the countless merchants, there are also entertainers like jugglers, fortune tellers, and magicians.

With the completion of the Waisenhaus and the prospect of a free social gathering, everyone appears to be happy. That is, until they actually hear the fortuneteller's omen.

Charis is a thin older woman with long silver hair tied neatly into a braid that hangs over her right shoulder. She has a very pretty face and grayed-over eyes indicating her state of total blindness. Alongside her is a younger man, presumably her son, who assists in managing her affairs.

Among the townsfolk, the old fortuneteller is seen as a communal grandmother who offers guidance without charging for her counsel, only seeking donations when they can be afforded.

Though otherwise of a calm demeanor, Charis is visibly upset this evening. She dismisses requests for insight on love and gardening, focusing instead on more pressing matters. Tonight, all she can speak of is a dark lord who has wrought a great deception and is now living among the townsfolk.

"He is unlike the rest of us!" she screeches. "The dark one will rise to amass terrible power and enslave the lot of you . . . unless we stop him!"

Emmerich begins to wonder . . . The boy knows he is different and will one day be strong like his mother. Is he the dark lord in her warning? Would he really enslave anyone?

Before he can answer, a tall man in a cape howls "Who wants to see some magic?!?"

"We do!" the crowd erupts, eager to be mystified by the supernatural being.

There is great anticipation for the magician's act. Though festivals were fairly consistent year-to-year, the entertainment was usually limited to local acts. This is the first year the traveling magician would be added to the program.

"What trick would you like to see?" he prompts the animated crowd.

~ A Celebration ~

"The rope . . . The handkerchief!" some blurt randomly, having had a sneak peek during setup.

"I know some tricks! I can perform magic!" yells Emmerich.

The magician ignores his comments and continues to press the villagers for their requests.

"I'm a wizard!" the young boy finally yells over the other children's voices.

The traveling magician laughs as do the others around him.

"Of course you are. What an active imagination!" he sneers loudly.

"For your first act . . . what say you conjure a pair of shoes?!?"

"Haa! Haa!," roars the crowd, laughing and pointing in his direction.

Emmerich looks down at his bare feet and borrowed clothes. They were laughing at him, not with. He slumps his shoulders and sits quietly towards the rear of the audience for the remainder of the show.

~ My Dragon Mother: The Dragon's Cup ~

Claudia notices the boy's withdrawn demeanor and slowly shuffles towards her clearly distraught friend. She tries to distract Emmerich by getting him to think of something more positive.

"Do you miss your mother?" she asks.

Emmerich nods silently without making eye contact.

"What is she like?" she prompts, trying to take his mind off of the magician's biting remarks.

"She's amazing," he says with a spark of enthusiasm. "Her beauty is unmatched in the entire world."

"Wow, she must be dazzling," encourages Claudia.

"That's an understatement," Emmerich assures her as he adjusts his posture. "She is very tall, has emerald green eyes, and has the most amazing smile."

"Like yours?" she asks.

Emmerich rubs his thumb against his teeth, landing upon his right canine. He recalls the size of

~ A Celebration ~

his mother's jaws and the flickering flame that highlights her protruding fangs.

"No, not like mine -- her teeth are bright like the stars above us."

Just then, a tall juggler appears dressed in a single-piece white outfit and begins to amaze the crowd with his acrobatic feats.

Throwing a red ball high into the air, the slender juggler shouts "One ball . . . then two . . . now three . . ."

With each count, the amazing juggler continues adding balls into the rotation, building suspense in his awestruck audience. The balls flow high and fast, forming a blurred oval as he contemplates adding another.

"Can he juggle four?!?" he calls into question as he signals to his assistant for the final ball.

"Yes!"

The crowd roars with applause as he continues the circular motion of colored orbs hurling through the air at his command.

~ My Dragon Mother: The Dragon's Cup ~

Claudia and Emmerich make their way to join a group of children sitting towards the front and watch as he performs unbelievable feats of balance and strength.

In closing his act, the juggler hurls his last object in the form of a question onto his audience "Who among you wants to be part of the show?"

The children rise and step towards their jubilant leader. In fact, Emmerich can no longer see as it appears that every hand was raised directly within his line of sight.

"I do!" they scream in unison as they eagerly rush towards the mixed pile of circus supplies.

The juggler passes out a variety of objects among the children. Some just hold them and march in place. Others attempt to juggle the items as he did; however, none are able to match his technique.

By the time Emmerich stands up, all of the juggler's props had been distributed, leaving him unable to participate in the festivities. Noticeably disappointed, he looks around for something else to do.

~ A Celebration ~

"I know," he mutters to himself.

Emmerich runs swiftly over to the main bonfire and gazes deep into its roaring center, his eyes widening with each dancing flicker. He assumes his 'attention stance' and focusing intently, rotates his arms in a wide circular motion exactly as he had witnessed in the juggler's act.

He then reaches his little hands into the enormous blaze and pulls fist-sized flashes from within its burning pit.

"One fire ball," he quietly mutters to himself, "then two."

As his arms continue to rotate, so do the golden balls of flame until they form a massive ring of fire. The pair of flashes climbs higher into the night sky, drawing the attention of nearby spectators.

"Now three," he continues with a rush of adrenaline as the flaming circle takes on a more solid appearance. "Can he juggle four?!?"

"No!"

The circle scatters and the flashes it once

contained suddenly fall from the sky like meteors. They land with a thump on and around the novice juggler's miniature frame.

"Awe -- I almost had it!" he exclaims, not immediately noticing the lack of activity that followed.

Only then does he recognize the faces of his friends and neighbors staring at him in a disturbed silence. They recall the fortuneteller's foreboding words about the 'dark lord' hiding among them.

"Perhaps Fulco was right in trying to be rid of this homeless foreigner," some thought to themselves.

"Perhaps we misjudged the young Baron when he was merely unsuccessful in completing his task," others say aloud.

Emmerich quietly extinguishes the flames and looks to Claudia for her support.

"What's the matter?" he asks with a worried expression, "Why is everyone looking at me?"

Before she could answer, Andreas and his

~ A Celebration ~

men approach the young wizard.

"Grab him!" commands their captain.

The soldiers look nervously towards each other for reassurance before proceeding.

"What if he hurls fire at them?" they think to themselves.

Overcoming their fear, the soldiers seize upon the boy's tiny frame and lift him high above their heads with arms outstretched as they carry him from away public view.

Once out of sight, they lock him in a distant stable used mainly for keeping beasts of burden -- one with a particularly strong scent of feed and manure.

It is a dark and dirty place, but for now, it will have to suffice -- at least until the council determines what to do with him.

Chapter IX

The Plan

Emmerich sits alone in the dark wondering what is to become of him. He is very tired and extremely sad, knowing that the townspeople think him to be some sort of monster.

"They believe I am the dark lord in the fortuneteller's warning," he sighs in incredulity. "Even my friends in the courtyard think I mean to harm them."

~ The Plan ~

The overwhelmed child wants desperately to leave this place but dares not teleport for fear that his life's energy may drop even further. All he wants is to be with his family. Sadly, that is something that is going to have to wait.

Emmerich looks about his surroundings to gauge whether there were any openings through which he could fit. As the young boy scans the dingy stable, he spies a large hole in its ceiling, giving him a clear view of the midnight sky.

He walks directly underneath it and peers through to gaze upon the rising moon, watching it fade and glow bright again as the cumulus clouds pass beneath it.

"Waxing Gibbous!" he gasps knowing the next phase in the cycle. "I don't have much time!" he exclaims with an intense feeling of dread coming over him.

The next full moon is at most a couple of days away, giving the budding wizard little time to feed and even less time for his mother to find him.

"She'll make it . . . She has to," Emmerich

whispers quietly with his eyes closed shut. "I know my mother will find me before it is too late."

Though hopeful of his mother's timely arrival, the young wizard's mind begins to fill with doubt along with the most desperate of mortal thoughts. He finds himself suddenly overwhelmed with the prospect of his imminent demise and the presumably unpleasant manner in which it would occur.

"What if they don't make it in time?" he wonders, "What will happen to me when the full moon sets? Will I whither into decay or simply fall listless into a permanent sleep?"

His disheartening thoughts continue to race one after another. Yet somehow Emmerich manages to calm himself and focuses instead on planning his immediate escape. In doing so, he notices an old horse resting in the adjacent stable.

"Excuse me horse . . . I don't mean to disturb your sleep," he says as he approaches the recovering beast of burden, "but I am trapped and need to get away. Can you help me get out of here?"

The old horse raises its head and turns

~ The Plan ~

towards the intruding child. "I have heard of humans who could speak to others beyond their own kind," he says in astonishment, "but, I never really thought it could happen. How is it that we are able to understand each other?"

"My name is Emmerich and I am a wizard," he states, introducing himself. "I mean, someday I hope to be a full one," he adds.

"I am Anzo," the old labor horse replies. "I have never met a wizard and am delighted to meet one at last," he says.

"Can you help me find a way out of here?" asks the boy.

"That's a lot to ask of anyone," Anzo replies, "especially of one so old and weak. All I can do these days is pull a plow, and that just barely."

The old horse looks away from the boy.

"Tell me, what good could that possibly do someone in your circumstance?"

Emmerich is disappointed in Anzo's response; not for the lack of assistance, but for the lack of self-worth in his rusty voice. The young boy refrains from expressing his feelings of discontent and instead offers the disheartened horse his mother's sage advice.

"I know what it is like to feel weak and helpless," he says gently. "I use to feel that way because I only saw myself from the outside and not from within."

Emmerich steps closer and brushes Anzo's mane. "Let me tell you what I see . . ."

The boy then places his hand upon the horse's head and closes his eyes. All of a sudden, a rush of Anzo's memories starts to channel directly into the young wizard's mind.

"You were once in the service of Schön's cavalry," he says watching a young Anzo march in the town's armed force.

Emmerich flashes through a collage of episodes from Anzo's life; including an array of battles, parades, and training regimens. The tour ends with a scene showing a wounded horse struggling to keep up with the rest of his formation.

~ The Plan ~

"When you were no longer able to carry the armored soldiers," he observes. "They moved you here to work in the fields."

The old horse drops his head, thus closing the mental bridge between them. He is ashamed that Emmerich had seen his former glory and now witnesses the remnants of a shattered being.

"Raise your head high," insists the boy, "for you have led a noteworthy life full of purpose."

"How could you say that, looking at the feeble mess I have become?" asks Anzo in disbelief.

Emmerich smiles and pets his new friend firmly on the back.

"Long ago, you defended these people with your service in battle and now you feed them through your efforts in the field," he asserts. "How else would they eat if not for the pulling of your plow?"

Anzo lifts his head once more, this time with a sense of pride.

"I never saw it that way," he confesses. "All

this time, I have lived in shame for not being able to fulfill my former duties. In pulling my plow, I now know that I am not a lowly creature after all, but the provider of many."

Anzo then looks towards Emmerich and declares, "It is because of you that my outlook, hence, my world has changed. I shall carry this sense of worth for the remainder of my days," he states, "and if I can help you, then I most definitely shall."

In completing his proclamation, Anzo shifts his gaze up towards the rafters.

"We are not alone," he says.

Just then, the young boy feels a soft ripple brush against the bottom of his foot.

"Herman!" exclaims Emmerich, recognizing the change in hue of the ground beneath.

The young gnome's translucent waves enter the dreary stable, ebbing and flowing like the tide. At its center rises the spirit figure of a gnome, calm and still as the earth from which it emerges.

"I am so happy to see you!" exclaims

~ The Plan ~

Emmerich, "Are you here to save me?"

Herman's peaceful demeanor is suddenly disrupted as he begins to hyper-ventilate, which is particularly odd since he is currently in his spirit, rather than physical, form.

"Save you?!? What's the matter? Are you okay?" asks Herman.

"Of course not! You're not okay!" he cries. "You're alone in a distant village full of strangers we don't even know! How could you possibly be okay?!?"

Herman then lunges towards Emmerich, falling through his body in an attempt to hold onto it.

"I should know better than to ask -- These things are obvious. If you were doing well, you would ask something like 'how are you feeling' instead of whether I was coming to YOUR RESCUE!"

"Relax Herman, I am not hurt," Emmerich tells him, ". . . just locked away for a bit."

Herman is relieved to see that the young

wizard is unharmed. Aside from actually caring for the boy, the gnome knows that saving Emmerich is his only chance of restoring his honor.

"How far away are you?" asks the young boy, hopeful that they were just over the next hill or two.

"At the rate we're going, we should reach you sometime tomorrow night," Herman tells him. "Of course, I am totally freaking out about the whole 'feed by the light of the full moon thing', but your mother is confident in being able to reach you in time."

"That's a relief," sighs Emmerich with a hopeful grin, "but wait," he blurts suddenly. "There are soldiers here -- lots of them! Please tell her to be careful."

"Don't worry about a thing regarding your rescue," Herman says in a confident tone, "It would take an army twice their size to even stand a chance against a dragon of her caliber."

"But she has gotten so weak," Emmerich mumbles as he kneels, feeling a sense of blame for her frail condition, "ever since she started feeding

~ The Plan ~

me."

"Don't blame yourself for her choices," Herman tells him, awkwardly patting through Emmerich's shoulder. "She wouldn't do it if she didn't love you."

Suddenly, they hear the sound of gravel shifting outside the stable as if someone had landed sharply upon it.

"Someone has jumped from the rooftop!" cries Herman, rising through the intruder's footprint. He returns to the stable and continues. "It is an armored man and he is swiftly running towards what appears to be the town's center."

It was Andreas! He had been spying on the boy from the rafters and heard their entire conversation.

"You must go!" Emmerich demands.

"But, how will I know if . . ."

"Go . . . and hurry!" yells Emmerich, fearing for what Andreas might do to him or his mother with this newfound knowledge.

~ My Dragon Mother: The Dragon's Cup ~

"The sooner you leave, the sooner you'll get here!" he tells him. "It's only a day -- I'll just have to figure something out for the time being."

***

Meanwhile, Andreas sprints as fast as his feet could carry his heavy, armor-laden frame; his mind racing frantically alongside him as he dashes to reach his fellow council members.

"I knew there was something off with that boy and now I know his secret!"

Andreas begins to wonder what it must be like to wield fire as easily as the young foreigner and conjures a myriad of ways for how he could use this skill in the field of combat.

"Once I have secured his power," he mutters with a smile on his face, "I'll have the strength to vanquish all of our enemies. But first, there's the matter of overcoming that dragon."

Just then, the invigorated captain of the guard arrives at the town center and opens the hall doors with both of his arms at once, drawing the immediate attention of the few who were patiently waiting

~ The Plan ~

inside.

"I bring vital news of the miraculous sort!" he proclaims proudly, raising his hands triumphantly above his head. He proceeds to recite the conversation he overheard in the stable; emphasizing keenly that the dragon was on its way.

"How is this good news?!?" asks Raban with a sneer, "We have a nuisance locked in a stable and an angry dragon the size of a house speeding towards our village to save him. What makes you think we can even defeat her in a fight?"

"My dear friend, things are not as dire as you make them out to be," Andreas assures him with a gentle pat on the cheek. "The beast does not suspect any danger and solely intends to 'feed him' when she arrives. That is our advantage!"

Turning towards the remainder of his peers, he adds "You saw what he did with the fire. Who knows what other great and terrible powers she would bestow upon him that fateful night?"

No one offers their captain any support, conveying instead a sense of reluctance on their part.

~ My Dragon Mother: The Dragon's Cup ~

"This boy is too young and weak to have earned such a magnificent force." he says. "We on the other hand have sculpted an ideal society and should be rewarded with even greater might!"

There is a brief period of silence as each of the council members carefully considers the warrior's proposal and the impact of wielding such power.

"We should get rid of the boy," offers Othmar. "With him gone, the dragon would have no reason to track him to us."

Sensing Andreas' apparent displeasure with his response, Othmar continues, "Plus, we have no need for such illusions. We are a mighty nation with a capable guard and impenetrable armor. We could easily defend ourselves if attacked."

"And miss the opportunity of a generation?!?" taunts Andreas. "With the dragon's might in both flesh and nourishment, we would reign supreme and rid for ourselves even the idea of a foreign invasion!"

Andreas is frustrated by his colleagues as demonstrated by the unconsciously clenched fist he now bears.

~ The Plan ~

"He has a point," chimes Mathildis much to Andreas' delight. "If the beast can transfer such power to a mere child, think of what could be done when we wield its strength."

Tied in a stalemate, Raban and Othmar aren't convinced and look to Tancred for his direction on how to proceed.

"We Bavarii are a prosperous people who value strength for the safety it provides us," he asserts while rising from his chair. "We would be remiss to pass on such a divine gift, for surely it is providence due to the lifestyle we have chosen."

His words resonate loudly with his peers and a sense of unity finally prevails over the council.

Tancred continues . . .

"In a day's time, we will trap this beast and feed abundantly from it, shaping a new era in our illustrious lineage."

He then places his arms over the shoulders of both Othmar and Andreas, looking towards Mathildis and Raban to join them in a huddle.

~ My Dragon Mother: The Dragon's Cup ~

"Let us join our talents in preparation for this impossible feat, for brawn alone will not suffice to seize our nation's destiny."

***

Later, back at the stable, Emmerich hears his name being called in a hushed manner. He looks around for signs that someone had entered, but does not see any proof of a visitor.

The boy then crouches to get a sideways view of the ground in case there were any translucent waves traveling across it.

"Herman?" he asks crossly, believing his instructions were clear for the gnome to continue on his journey.

"Who's Herman?" asks the squeaky voice in a confused tone.

Emmerich determines the voice's direction and looks up to identify the source of the sound. He immediately recognizes the heads of Claudia and Fulco partially blocking the setting moon.

"What is HE doing here?" asks Emmerich.

~ The Plan ~

"We're both here to rescue you," Claudia explains while lowering a rope down to her captive friend. "Now hurry before we get caught."

"Why would you do something nice for me?" he asks suspiciously, glaring intensely at the boy who tried to burn him.

There is a brief pause as Fulco collects his thoughts. He is clearly struggling with the conflict of explaining his suddenly noble behavior, especially to his nemesis.

"Look . . . You saved our lives, so we're saving yours," Fulco explains curtly. "Now climb up here before those guards suspect what we're doing.'

With time ticking, Emmerich doesn't have much of a choice. He motions to Anzo and asks if he could give him a lift.

Anzo leaves his stall and centers himself below the dangling cord that before now was simply too high for the young boy to reach. Emmerich thanks him and begins to climb, steadily making his way towards the ceiling.

At the rope's end, the weary youth summons

every bit of his strength to help squeeze through the jagged hole in the roof. He then looks back down into the stable and waves at his four-legged friend.

"Now what?" Emmerich asks, hoping a robust plan had been laid out by his rescuers.

"We leave, of course," gestures Claudia with a puzzled expression.

"That's it?" he thinks to himself, not feeling much better about his chances for survival.

Emmerich is grateful for at least getting out of his temporary prison. At least now he has a chance of escaping and can hopefully avoid a confrontation with his captors.

"But, where?" he asks delicately, trying not to offend his friend while still prodding for a bit more detail.

The children pause as they think of where to hide their companion. Whatever their destination, it would only be required for a short while since Emmerich's mother was already on her way.

~ The Plan ~

"I know just the place," says Fulco as he leads them down the back of the building.

~ My Dragon Mother: The Dragon's Cup ~

Chapter X

A Beautiful Place

Fulco makes his way down from the rooftop and helps both Claudia and Emmerich reach the ground with soft, inaudible landings. He then safely leads his companions away from the dingy stable and starts walking towards the more ominous woods.

"Where are you taking us?" asks Emmerich with a tinge of distrust.

"Schön is no longer safe," Fulco declares.

~ A Beautiful Place ~

"The guards will search every building until you are found. Then, who knows what will happen," he states in a dark, menacing tone.

Fulco then points far into the distance, spotting the highest peak in the Bavarii range. He calls Claudia's and Emmerich's attention to a large snow-capped mountain shining brightly in the moon light.

"We should go to Mount Watzmo," he insists. "There you will have shelter and be able to see if anyone is coming."

The location looks fine from where Emmerich is standing. It is far from the village and appears to be isolated enough to where he could safely reunite with his family.

In viewing the landscape, he notices the rough terrain and steep edges that make up the mountain's facade. The young boy accepts this as being his best available course of action, but feels uncomfortable dragging his companions along on this perilous trek.

"What about Claudia?" Emmerich whispers secretly to Fulco.

"You can go home now," Fulco asserts while motioning the young girl back towards the village. "We'll manage things from here."

"What do you mean, I can go?!?" Claudia asks indignantly. "I brought the rope!" she exclaims.

"The rope has served its purpose and so have you," Fulco replies.

"So what if we did," she replies indignantly. "If anyone should go home, it should be you -- as you're the only one with parents waiting for him."

Claudia's own comment catches her off-guard. She takes a few breaths to keep her tears from flowing down her cheeks.

"My parents are gone," she says looking down sadly into her palms, "but yours will surely know you are missing. What if they blame Emmerich for your disappearance and go after him?"

"No . . . They won't," sighs Fulco. "The paths would be too numerous and dangerous for a meaningful pursuit."

Emmerich and Claudia look puzzled towards

~ A Beautiful Place ~

each other.

"It's only in front of others that my mother and father act as if they really care for me," Fulco continues with a miserable expression. "The rest of the time, they act like I am not even there."

Emmerich looks to Claudia, assuring her it was okay to turn back. She shakes her head furiously and signals to move forward.

"You'll definitely get caught if we just keep standing here," she says tersely, gesturing again to move in their intended direction.

The two boys nod in unison, acknowledging her logic and immediately embark upon their perilous trek; one that would lead them through a dizzying trail of dirt, ice, and rock.

The path out of town is surprisingly easy. All they have to do is follow the banks of the Königssee, a grand sapphire lake at the base of the Bavarii Alps.

By wading through the Königssee's shoreline waters, their trail of tiny footprints is erased almost immediately after their impressions are first made. With no way to track them, the children's quest takes on a noticeably more jubilant mood.

As dawn breaks, the sun's rays quietly announce the arrival of their master, splitting the sky into light and dark realms joined together by a delightful pink-blue tint that conforms to neither.

The enchanting moment promotes a sense of serenity among the children. For even without the comforts of food and rest, it is hard for them not to enjoy their hike with such a beautiful panorama. It turns out that Emmerich really did find the most beautiful place in the entire world.

"Whoa!" exclaims Emmerich. "What is that?!?"

"That is the glacier guard that stands between the forest and Mount Watzmo," explains their guide, "It was placed there by the gods when our people descended from its lofty peak."

Claudia and Emmerich were truly astounded by what they saw. High above them, in line with the tall firs and pines, stood a massive glacier too large to view with a single glance. Its jagged edges and smooth walls made the towering structure

~ A Beautiful Place ~

impenetrable, clearly dissuading any sane person from climbing its enormous facade.

"Glacier Guard?" asks Emmerich, continuing to stare in awe at the mammoth block of ice.

"Shift your eyes upwards and gaze upon the face of my ancestors," Fulco instructs proudly as he points to an immense armed sentinel carefully carved into the side of the primordial glacier.

Emmerich follows his instruction and sees a giant bearded guard fashioned in full battle attire and brandishing a mighty spear. The silent, frosted figure stands ever vigilant, looking menacingly down towards any would-be intruders to keep them away from his people's ancient birthplace.

It is truly extraordinary to witness such an ancient carving that has withstood the destructive passage of time. With a blue-green hue emanating from within the glacier's solid core, the colossus appears to be of the ethereal rather than a mere statue.

"How do we get through it?" asks Claudia. "There's no place to step on or grab onto," she proclaims in despair.

"You can follow me. There's a passage right over here," says Fulco, motioning to a hidden staircase behind the frosty figure.

"The town elders consider this place sacred and warn never to trespass, but I come here all the time," he boasts. "I know all of the secret passages along with the best places to hide."

Claudia is impressed with Fulco's leadership and knowledge and eagerly follows him up the stairs.

"Come on!" she yells down towards Emmerich, encouraging him to follow.

Emmerich stares at the icy surface and then back at his bare feet. He bends down to touch it with his hand and feels a cold sting run straight through his fingertips. The young boy looks up into the dark staircase and hears that Fulco and Claudia have already reached the top.

"What if I just teleport?" he thinks to himself in an attempt to avoid the frost. "With less than a day to go, I simply can't chance it. What if I don't make it or wind up someplace else?"

~ A Beautiful Place ~

The young boy takes a deep breath and steps onto the frozen staircase, cringing as it burns the bottom of his exposed feet.

"Just keep moving Emmerich," calls Fulco from up above. "It will get easier."

Emmerich reaches the staircase's end and is greeted by a bright white sheet of ice flanked by a clear blue sky. Meanwhile, his companions are peering over the glacier's sharp edge trying to determine the height they had just scaled.

"Come on, Emmerich," encourages Fulco, placing his arm around the shivering youth. "Let's get you off this block of ice and onto someplace warmer."

He then points towards the top of the awaiting mountain and says, "There are caves up there where you will be safe. We just need to get past this section and you're home free. Be sure to stay close and we'll make it there -- together."

Emmerich nods and begins walking in the direction Fulco indicated. As he makes his way across the barren terrain, the rising sun proves unable to warm him and the frigid trail increasingly more difficult.

With each step, the improperly dressed boy feels increasingly strong aches in his toes, ankles, and shins. Midway through his ordeal, he winces in pain as the glacier's frosty grip reaches up just past his knees and firmly unto his lower back.

Emmerich keeps his eyes closed, wondering again whether he should just teleport and be done with this pointless suffering -- one way or another. He inhales deeply, thereby controlling his breath in an attempt to focus his strength, but is suddenly distracted by an alarming sound.

"Careful!" yells Fulco, grabbing Claudia by the back of her cardigan. He then pulls her towards him as the ice where she previously stood collapses suddenly into a gaping abyss.

"Thanks, I owe you one," whispers Claudia beneath her breath. She is clearly shaken up by what would have been her early demise and clings momentarily to Fulco's side.

"They're so unpredictable, cracking and

~ A Beautiful Place ~

breaking with the slightest bit of pressure," he states with a contented smile for earning her affection. "We should keep moving. The cracking gets worse as the sun warms the glacier's surface."

With no place to rest, the young caravan presses until it reaches the base of the mountain. In doing so, the young wizard's once cheery stride degrades until it resembles more of a hobble.

"I really need to stop!" Emmerich exhales in anguish. He sits at the edge of the mountain's giant shadow for a brief moment and rubs his feet with both hands, trying desperately to regain some of their lost heat and sensation.

"Come on Emmerich, it is just a little further," yells Fulco, waving his arms in the air as if crossing a finish line. "That thin ledge is all that remains between you and a warm fire!"

Claudia then pulls Emmerich by the arms and helps him rise to his feet. "You can do it," she says in an encouraging tone. "We must be close by now as I can no longer see the top of Mount Watzmo."

Emmerich looks up towards the mountain

top and is stunned by its imposing face. She is right -- the top is no longer visible but then again, neither is Fulco.

"Fulco!" they yell into the looming void.

Fulco runs back into view and reasserts that the trail's end is drawing near. He points into the distance, where they can faintly see a series of caves hovering high above the glacier.

Feeling a sense of renewal, Emmerich picks up the pace of his crippled gait with the hope of feeling warmth once more. He climbs the ledge with all of his remaining strength, gripping the side of the mountain to keep from sliding down again.

The path is treacherous with slick surfaces that seem to narrow with each additional step, making it extremely difficult to maintain a grip. In making a turn, Emmerich slips and catches himself, watching the rubble fall down the side of the mountain.

"That's a long way down," he thinks to himself. "There's no way I'd survive the fall."

Upon reaching the cavern, Fulco and Claudia

~ A Beautiful Place ~

rush inside, eager to explore. Meanwhile, Emmerich collapses and waits for the stinging in his legs to subside.

"This is incredible!" exclaims Claudia. "How long have you been coming here?"

She points to a myriad of drawings increasingly made visible as Fulco ignites torches across the cavern walls. Each tells a tale of its own, ranging from hunting excursions to full military campaigns.

"These are clearly from another time," she thinks to herself, wondering if perhaps an ancestor of hers had fashioned the vase she was holding.

With the cave fully illuminated, the three children gather at its center and relish in having beaten the elements. Emmerich recovers slowly from his frosty aches amid the warmth of a roaring fire and the nurturing feelings of friendship. They reflect upon their hazardous journey and take turns sharing their darkest moments in addition to their favorite scenes.

The sun sets and the amber glow of the

torches matches the serenity felt by the young trio. Their bond has grown strong and the grievances of their past appear to melt away like the ice crystals that followed them inside.

As the conversation dwindles, Claudia yawns as she strokes a deep clay bowl she found near the cave's central altar.

"I'm getting hungry," she says.

"Me too," agrees Fulco, looking towards a barren table with chairs thrown about.

Suddenly, their peace is disrupted by the crash of armor amid shuffling footsteps.

"Don't fret, my dear . . . Mommy's here!" sings Mathildis as she enters the cave.

~ My Dragon Mother: The Dragon's Cup ~

Chapter XI

The Storm Within

"What did you do?!?" screams Claudia, glaring furiously at her deceiver.

Fulco is caught off guard by her sudden change in disposition.

Just a few brief moments ago, they were fast becoming friends that shared a sense of comradery and acceptance. Now, he barely recognizes her as she appears absolutely wild with anger.

~ My Dragon Mother: The Dragon's Cup ~

"My son did what any descent Bavarii would have done," Mathildis assures the distraught young girl, gently stroking her long wavy hair, "at least one with a proper upbringing."

Mathildis then flings Claudia's hair away from her and commands, "Now calm down while we get things sorted."

She then walks past the bewildered children, bringing with her a group of heavily armored soldiers. Her fellow council members follow soon there-after, looking about the prehistoric dwelling in anticipation of their impending battle.

"What are you going to do with me?" asks Emmerich, rising to his feet, clearly exhausted from his difficult journey.

Mathildis crouches down and faces Emmerich while her co-conspirators start rearranging the cavern contents, completely ignoring the young trio.

"You?" she smirks, caressing his hollow cheek. "What on Earth would we want with you?"

Mathildis then grips Emmerich firmly by the jaw and, in a menacing tone, says, "It is your vile

~ The Storm Within ~

beast of a mother that we want."

Emmerich pushes her hand away from his face and shouts, "Don't call her that!"

The young boy stares angrily at Mathildis and starts to ponder what he could do to make her sorry for her offense.

The wicked woman senses his naivety and continues to press further.

"Oh . . . Would you rather another name for your darling dragon?!" she taunts with a mischievous smile. "How about animal, creature, or monster?" she says flicking her wrists with every offensive word.

Emmerich is shocked and cannot think of what to say in his mother's defense. He had never before heard such despicable expressions directed at someone he loved so dearly.

With Emmerich sulking, Claudia consoles her fragile friend and then turns aggressively once more towards Fulco.

"What is wrong with you?" she grumbles. 'He saved your life and this is how you repay him? How can you stand being so despicable?"

"Wrong with me? You're the one who is friends with a freak!" he yells, turning to see the commotion at the altar.

"Besides," he continues, "you would have done the same if you had anything or anyone worth fighting for."

Claudia stares at him in silence. Through their journey, she had come to appreciate his kinder, gentler side and even allowed herself to be vulnerable in his presence. She never anticipated that he would use her deepest insecurities against her.

And though Fulco only meant part of what he said, each of his words found a target deep within Claudia's being, leaving her wilted and lame in spirit.

Soon after, a hush falls over the crowd as Andreas prepares to speak. He is a brilliant leader and commands the attention even of his detractors. Everybody listens in silence.

"Tonight, we stand at the dawn of a new era," he says as if announcing his victory. "By the setting of the full moon, we will possess a power so great

~ The Storm Within ~

that none of our enemies would dare offend us."

His soldiers lift their swords and spears high into the air, indicating a willingness to follow their captain in the pursuit of his magnificent vision.

"There is but one obstacle," he continues. "A mere beast is all that stands between us and security of our home."

The soldiers laugh as they gauge their strength in numbers when matched against a single creature, regardless of its ferocity.

"If we fail, then it won't be long until the Bavarii become a conquered and forgotten people," Andreas continues soberly. "But if we succeed, then we shall become the most powerful nation . . . not just in the world, but also in its history!"

The Bavarii delegation cheers with delight and channels its energy towards seizing their glorious destiny. After all, Andreas had proven to be a remarkable military strategist and his plan to trap the mighty dragon was already being referred to as his best idea yet.

"One way in . . . No way out!" the soldiers

mutter, feeling practically assured of their triumph.

His troupe spends hours preparing for their impending conquest and build precisely to his specifications. They rearrange the gloomy environment and build a massive structure to ensnare their celebrated catch.

***

Later . . . as the full moon approaches the peak of Mount Watzmo, a sense of calm envelopes the largely dormant landscape.

On any other night, a dark sky would bring about few noteworthy things, limited to the mundane light from the moon or stars. But tonight, there is something more mystical in the air as the clock strikes midnight.

High above the Schön skyline, there are two green dots flickering in the distance. At first, it would appear that they were stars like any other. But stars don't rise in the west and they definitely don't grow larger the longer you stare at them. No, these are the eyes of a dragon and they are searching for something dear.

~ The Storm Within ~

It has been a long strenuous journey and Leona has flown practically nonstop in search of her son. She is tired and weak but perseveres to once more see his smile and feel his warm embrace. Emmerich is in imminent danger and she has only a few precious moments to save him.

The female dragon surveys the area below, looking for obvious signs of aggression. Being cautious, she lands in a patch of forest across the lake from the township and asks Herman to find her son.

"Find him," she urges her young companion. "Emmerich is running out of energy and will soon have to replenish his strength."

The young gnome dismounts the dragon and closes his eyes, binding his heartbeat to nature's singular rhythm. He barely hears the first complete heartbeat when his eyes begin to twitch. Then, in an almost jerking fashion, he opens them quickly once more.

"He's up there!" he shouts pointing at the mountain, feeling a rush of excitement for being so close to his redemption, "He is in a large cave located just below the peak."

~ My Dragon Mother: The Dragon's Cup ~

Leona motions for Herman to climb aboard so they may rush towards her little boy.

"There are more," he continues, "I sense two other young ones at his side . . . but something's not right."

"What is it?" she asks in an irritated tone, knowing that any time wasted would likely cost her son his life.

"I can't explain it, but they seem overly tense for their age." he says with a confused expression. "I could go there and confirm, but it's going to take me a while to get through all of that rock."

"Climb on!" commands Leona. "We don't have much time."

She takes to the air and speeds towards the awaiting cave on Mount Watzmo. As they near their destination, Herman continues to voice his sense of worry and discomfort.

"Emmerich mentioned soldiers the last time we spoke," he recounts, "What if this uneasy feeling means it's some sort of trap?"

~ The Storm Within ~

"Then we'll deal with it when we get there," Leona replies with piercing determination.

A brief moment later, Leona dives through the cave entrance, extinguishing half of the light within it. As she shifts her weight, the dim torch light bounces off of her shimmering scales, projecting a dark menacing glare throughout the cave's interior.

"Emmerich! Come to me . . . quickly!" she cries, looking for him frantically in the dark.

Sensing his lack of motion, she turns to see several dozen soldiers standing atop chairs and benches, poised to attack. It's no wonder Herman couldn't see them. The furniture's lifeless limbs had lost all touch with nature once they were twisted by the race of men.

She tries to move, but finds it difficult to even adjust her weight. Leona exhales a breath of flame and sheds light upon her surroundings.

To her astonishment, she is trapped in a structure of iron and wood built in preparation for her arrival. It contains a converging series of spears all pointing in a single direction, like a massive cone -- only with sharp edges as opposed to smooth ones.

"Don't move, Leona!" yells Herman as he climbs out of the piercing trap, "The blades are nestled between your scales."

Leona knows he is right. She could easily continue to move forward, but then feels the pinch of iron when she tries to move back. The dragon refrains from advancing further as she could clearly see the terminal end of her captor's trap -- a tight muzzle with hundreds of spikes intended to completely immobilize her.

Leona quickly shimmies backwards in an effort to escape, but is pierced on her sides by the razor-sharp enclosure.

"One way in . . . No way out!" Andreas' men chant towards their captive.

The Bavarii soldiers and their leaders roar in victory seeing that their once formidable prize is now unable to escape. Emboldened by the dragon's immobilized state, several soldiers approach their struggling prisoner in an attempt to draw her milk.

~ The Storm Within ~

"Get away from me!" Leona screams at the encroaching brigade.

The band of soldiers ignores her warning and proceeds to invade her personal space.

Leona suddenly flicks her horned tail and knocks the offending troupe clear out of the cavern, hurling them onto the jagged crater beneath. Their screams are heard long after they have ceased to be seen.

"Mother!" cries Emmerich.

Leona turns towards her son's innocent voice and notices a blade placed squarely against his throat. She is increasingly vexed, having travelled so far only to land in battle -- when all she wants is to feed her son.

"He's a talented one," flatters Tancred, pointing to a guard holding Emmerich by the tip of his sword. "We've seen what he can do with fire. Tell me, how well does he tolerate iron in his blood?"

"Cut him and I will scorch you," she threatens the hostile guard in a deep intimidating growl.

~ My Dragon Mother: The Dragon's Cup ~

The guard looks to his chieftain and reaffirms his grip, causing the little boy to gasp. Instinctively, Leona unleashes an inferno in his direction, melting even the sword that threatened her son. The guard screams as high as the flames that devour him, all while Emmerich remains unharmed.

As with Vulferam before, the young wizard simply watches as the flame travels across his body and pats out any remaining embers lingering upon his clothes.

Leona continues to expel flame and covers herself entirely with it. As the wood disintegrates, so does the integrity of the structure, quickly reducing the trap that once held her to little more than a smoldering pile of ash.

Meanwhile, Mathildis rushes to seize the young boy and pulls him close to her bosom. As Leona shakes off the remainder of the dust, Mathildis scrapes Emmerich on the chin with a bejeweled dagger.

"Woops!" she taunts the mighty dragon, as a trickle of blood races down his neck. "It seems I am quicker at drawing blood than even our own

~ The Storm Within ~

soldiers."

Emmerich struggles to escape but is unable to break free of Mathildis' grip. His frail and weakened body is simply no match for her unwavering frame.

"Try that with me and I'll skewer your little lamb chop," she says with a scowl, staring intently at the female dragon.

Leona takes a deep breath and prepares to roast her reckless adversary. She hesitates slightly only because of the glare in Mathildis' eyes. Where the guard had failed, this fiendish woman may actually succeed in hurting the little boy.

"All we want is your milk," blurts Raban in a desperate attempt to save Mathildis' life, "Let us draw from your well of power and we will release this bony scarecrow."

He then giggles aloud, looking for others to chime in, but is left alone to his chuckling.

"What would you do with it?" asks Leona, turning away from the impasse with Mathildis in favor of the laughing fool.

~ My Dragon Mother: The Dragon's Cup ~

"That business is our own!" calls Andreas from the far corner of the cavern, "Once we have your milk, you will be free to return to the wild with your son."

"How do I know you will honor this bargain?" the distraught mother asks suspiciously of her armored opponent.

"You have my word," Andreas states earnestly, "No harm shall come to you or the boy if you give us what we want."

Leona nods, fearing that a long impasse will only cause time to run out for her dilapidated child. She has traveled such a long way and now only wishes to leave with him -- safe and sound.

With the dragon's posture no longer in a fighting stance, the soldiers raise their swords in triumph and quickly approach the humbled dragon -- this time with shackles forged by Othmar.

"It is pointless to struggle," the supreme metallurgist says with absolute confidence, "This amalgam is laced with human suffering. Even the gods cannot be free of these chains."

~ The Storm Within ~

As the locks clamp down, the weight of the world literally falls upon Leona and drags her body to the ground. Unable to move in the slightest, the defeated dragon finally surrenders her breast plate.

Emmerich is instantly cast aside as Mathildis and the council advance to claim their prize. In their excitement, they and the soldiers conveniently forget their agreement and start to chastise the dragon, brutally striking about her helpless frame.

Emmerich watches helplessly through a veil of tears as his mother is repeatedly humiliated.

The young boy is unable to stop them as they proceed to treat her in the manner as she was earlier described . . . an animal, a creature, a monster.

~ My Dragon Mother: The Dragon's Cup ~

Chapter XII

Dark Tidings

As the Bavarii's wicked celebration begins to taper, Raban grabs a large clay bowl and rushes to place it beneath their magical prisoner.

Making his way towards the captive dragon, the town's high priest begins to sneer and walk in a peculiar manner, slouching and raising one shoulder higher than the other. He places the primitively decorated bowl upon his head like a jester and pitifully attempts to make the others laugh.

~ Dark Tidings ~

As usual, he just looks clumsy, leaving the others to wonder about his worthiness of being their tribe's spiritual leader.

"What is hers shall soon be ours!" he calls over the crowd, straightening his back into an upright posture. "When we drink of the beast, we shall be forever nourished and forget the likes of hunger, sickness, and death."

His message and sudden change in tone stun his audience into absolute silence. They remain quiet and attentive, insisting him to proceed.

"Cast aside your fear, my brothers," he says as he nears the dragon's breast plate. "Calm days and nights await the newer, stronger breed of Bavarii."

Raban's words comfort the crowd and dispel any lingering doubts they may have had about drinking the creature's milk. He had the knowledge of many things and was credible in navigating the commonly unknown, especially regarding the supernatural.

As the high priest prepares to draw the immortal elixir, Leona conveys a dire warning to her overly ambitious captors.

"You don't fully understand what you'll cause with your actions," she tells them in a grave tone.

Raban looks to Tancred and gestures his assurance that everything is in hand.

"Regret is a terrible thing," cautions Leona, "especially when it could have been prevented."

The priest pauses momentarily to ponder her paternal warning. Gauging the heightened anticipation of his fellow council members, he hastily scoffs at her prophetic words and directs the soldiers to stretch out her curled body.

She resists their efforts, causing them to struggle with her size and strength, but in the end her fatigue prevails over her will and she ultimately yields to their collective force.

"If it is protection you seek," she cries in a frantic tone, attempting to dissuade them, "then I shall give you the knowledge so that your people may always sleep comfortably at night!"

Tancred bursts into laughter, prompting the

others to do the same. He dismisses her plea, feeling it to be a lesser option than the one they already possess.

"Sleep?!?" he yells, squinting his eyes as if her had heard incorrectly. "Is that all you have to offer?"

"I don't know about you," he directs towards his comrades, looking about the cavern with his arms raised high in the air, "but I don't need lessons from a dimwitted brute to help me dream of a better life!"

The soldiers roar with excitement and urge their priest to continue, as do the other council members.

"You've heard them, Raban," the chieftain confirms, placing his hand upon the cleric's shoulder. "Proceed as planned."

"Wait!" yells Andreas, quickly stepping forward while gesturing for his colleague to stop in his tracks.

There was a deafening silence in the cavern. Without exception, they all wondered why their captain, the strongest among them, would suddenly hesitate to realize his own vision.

~ My Dragon Mother: The Dragon's Cup ~

Andreas senses their confusion and feels their collective glare penetrate him, almost hearing their disillusion with his single act of restraint.

Until that moment, all he could think of was the potential for limitless power and how he would ultimately wield it. At times, he even grew impatient knowing that such force was almost within his grasp.

Now that he stands at the cusp of immortality, he reflects on how this moment actually came to be and is ashamed of his actions.

In realizing his ambition, he had turned his otherwise remarkable troops into little more than an armed mob and shamelessly mistreated an innocent family, literally attacking a mother and her child.

This is not the image of the Bavarii he had fought to uphold and feels an urgent need to repent for his transgression.

Yet, there he stands with the creature he had personally abused just moments before -- one who still offers to help them even though she had recently suffered at their hands.

"What knowledge can you give us?" he

~ Dark Tidings ~

humbly asks Leona, loosening the chains that bind her.

"What does it matter?!?" exclaims an astonished Tancred.

Andreas looks up to see his chieftain quickly approaching.

"It's like you said," Tancred continues, stopping Andreas from further releasing their captive. "We have an opportunity to reclaim the birthright of our ancestors and descend from this mountain as gods!"

"I agree on the rarity of the opportunity," replies Andreas, "but what if her knowledge is equally as powerful?" Wouldn't it behoove us to learn her secrets as well?"

"You're missing the whole point, Andreas!" Tancred yells in frustration. "Through this creature, we shall reign supreme and rule over EVERY land -- not just our own pitiful patch!"

Just then, Andreas understands his chieftain's true intent. In doing so he slowly backs away, realizing the vast difference in their interpretations for the meaning and purpose of power.

Andreas stops and collects his thoughts. He can see the hostility in Tancred's eyes and attempts to reason with him.

"I only seek to protect our homes," he finally manages to say to him, "and have no desire for the spoils of conquest."

Tancred does not agree and stands firmly between Andreas and their prisoner to emphasize his unbending position.

"If we can achieve that end with the dragon's knowledge, then we should proceed to do so," he states, looking for the others to echo his sentiment.

The group divides . . . with Andreas on one end and Tancred on the other.

"Think of our people," he continues in his appeal. "Think of how we would all benefit from the shared learning."

Mathildis, Raban, and Othmar stare blankly at their converted dove and nod to each other in silence, opting to move in the direction of their

~ Dark Tidings ~

chieftain.

Andreas stands alone in his decision and can barely contain his disappointment.

"We would never have to fight another war," he says in a defeated tone. "We would finally know peace."

"Then it is settled," Tancred proclaims as the council members position themselves around him.

"Guards!" he calls to a group of soldiers. "Restrain your former captain until we have concluded our affairs."

Andreas is immediately detained and moved to a corner far away from the council's ceremony.

Raban then proceeds to draw milk from the dragon's breast plate and presents the bowl to his chieftain.

"Be the first to drink, my lord," he says in a tone reserved for only the highest of ceremonies, "and claim your place at the head of all tables."

Tancred closes his eyes and sips from the overflowing bowl, savoring the taste of victory in restoring his traditional birthright. As the thick and silky milk splashes against his lips, he blissfully acknowledges that his days of compromise are finally over. No longer would he suffer the indignation of having to appeal to others when expressing his divine will.

He then wipes his face and lifts the heavy bowl into the air, drawing cheers and applause from his fellow Bavarii.

"When the council is done drinking," he says handing the bowl back to Raban, "slay the beast!"

"No!" screams Emmerich, standing next to him.

The council had gone back on its promise and now his mother is going to die. The young wizard gauges the size difference between him and the soldiers and frowns in despair.

"I can't win," he sighs, wishing he was bigger, stronger -- anything that would save his mother.

Suddenly, he remembers his mother's words as if she were repeating them at that exact moment.

~ Dark Tidings ~

"Yes, you would be unsuccessful -- Not for the reasons you observed, but because you have yielded solely to the apparent and failed to recognize what is already inside of you."

As the remaining council members bask in their triumph, Emmerich frantically thinks of a way to defeat them.

He looks up towards the cavern wall and hones in on the numerous war scenes scribbled upon it. The young wizard envisions the battles taking place, watching the skinny stick figures race across the wall to defeat their equally thin adversaries.

He then starts stacking chairs and benches in an effort to reach the ceiling.

"Help me move these," he calls to Claudia and Herman. "I need to climb as high as possible."

"What are you doing?" asks Herman.

"You'll see," Emmerich tells the young gnome. "Just make a stack so I can climb it."

His two friends start throwing random items in haste. As the pile of furniture and pots continues to grow, the young boy makes his way above it, often slipping and crashing on the loose items below.

Emmerich reaches the very top of the unstable structure and removes his mother's claw tip from around his neck.

"I hope this works," he says to himself.

The young wizard starts to scratch furiously on the cavern wall, crossing uncontrollably over the prehistoric drawings that inspired him.

His etches begin to form lines that eventually turn into barely recognizable shapes. As he carves his drawing into the wall, his knuckles scrape against its jagged and tough surface, causing them to bruise and bleed. Even then, he continues to draw, smearing his own blood across the stone canvas.

"That should do it," Emmerich mutters as he finishes his colossal figure. "I may be small, but you are definitely not!"

He pauses briefly to admire his artwork -- a giant beast in the shape of a wild savage, scratched across numerous etchings that depict battles from long ago. He adds sharp claws, a large club, and jagged teeth to complete its arsenal.

~ Dark Tidings ~

Emmerich then utters in a breathy tone, "Erat Spiritus Vitae" and watches a small translucent figure jump from his lips, flex his arms, and dive straight into the cavern wall. The young wizard waits only briefly in anticipation for his rugged monster to spring to life.

The savage beast opens its eyes, blinks, and then tears itself away from the cavern wall, bellowing a bloodcurdling howl to announce its birth.

"Save my mother!" Emmerich commands, as his life's energy quickly begins to fade.

Emmerich falls to the ground as the beast moves swiftly to fulfill his master's orders. The boy is intent on saving his mother, even if it takes his final breath.

In the young boy's mind, this is not a senseless sacrifice. The way he sees it, he was as good as dead when Leona found him. She just delayed his passing, for which he is grateful.

As the beast approaches the altar, the Bavarii's eyes widen with astonishment and flee to escape its impending assault.

~ My Dragon Mother: The Dragon's Cup ~

The giant figure then lunges and swings its massive club, hurling a mass of soldiers in a single blow. The thumping of his feet is drowned out solely by the grinding of his teeth and the pleas for mercy that follow soon after.

In haste, the council members take turns to drink from the bowl with the supernatural beverage, feeling satisfied that their fates had finally been sealed.

Fulco tugs at his mother's sleeve and asks for a taste of his own. Mathildis lifts her hand and cruelly pushes him away.

"What would a child do with power?!?" she laughs with a wicked shrill, looking down at her son with contempt.

Fulco is shattered by his mother's betrayal. He always knew they weren't the most loving parents, but still thought they would include him in their life's journey.

"We are gods now and WE are no longer the same," she tells him. "You will serve your masters like the rest of your pathetic lot."

~ Dark Tidings ~

Just then, Emmerich's wild beast thrusts forward, scattering the tribal leaders and hurling the bowl of dragon's milk against the wall.

As they fall to the ground, their eyes darken to an impenetrable black, matching the opaqueness of their souls. Their skin drips off of their bodies and is replaced with a concoction of fur, feather, and bone. In doing so, they fiercely convulse as if they had fallen into some sort of unholy seizure.

The remaining soldiers look on in horror as their leaders warp into a herd of disfigured creatures. When the council members finally stop quaking, they stand and shake their ghastly heads.

Andreas' theory was correct in that they would indeed amass incredible power by drinking the dragon's milk. However, they had wrongly assumed that they would retain their external appearance like the child they witnessed at last night's festival.

Instead, the council is overwhelmed with the might of the immortal and ache in rage from their hideous transformation.

"I am a fiend," whispers Tancred in

bewilderment, looking down to examine his revolting hands and feet.

Mathildis, Raban, and Othmar then rise and look to each other in complete disgust. Meanwhile, Andreas and the few remaining soldiers look on in horror from across the cavern.

"Immortality?!?" Mathildis screams. "Who wants to look like this forever?"

Raban slowly raises his gruesome hands as if to guard himself from his cohorts.

"Easy now . . . We did drink the milk of a beast," he says in a snippy tone, indicating the apparently miserable outcome should have been at least partially expected.

His deformed colleagues do not appreciate his condescension and slowly move towards him to physically convey their sentiments.

"Perhaps you should worry less about our appearance," he continues, trying desperately to avoid a beating, "and focus instead on testing your newfound powers!"

~ Dark Tidings ~

"He's right!" shouts Tancred, furiously shaking his fists. "Let's see what kind of strength this fiend possesses."

He motions to Othmar and jointly seeks out the stone savage that decimated his army. If Tancred is to die today, then he would do so in battle with a truly legendary opponent. But if he were to defeat the colossus, then the legend to be told would be his own.

The two malformed brutes approach Emmerich's unsuspecting beast from the rear as it busily untangles the imprisoned Leona.

Tancred turns the rocky figure by the waist and punches straight through its left arm, promptly reducing the savage's stony limb to dust. Thrilled by the result, he and Othmar begin dismantling the boy's supernatural champion, relishing in the miraculous power they now possess.

With the beast fully vanquished, its borrowed breath escapes and immediately returns to Emmerich as he sits alone in a dilapidated state.

Sensing the boy's eminent demise, the council

members decide to share the misery they have personally inflicted. They turn their attention towards the motionless dragon and call out a dreadful proclamation.

"You have bewitched us, beast!" asserts Tancred. "For that, you will suffer; starting with the life of your son."

~ *My Dragon Mother: The Dragon's Cup* ~

Chapter XIII

Mother's Milk

Emmerich sits quietly by himself, feeling his life's force slipping further away with every additional breath. He is extremely weak and can barely understand the commotion at the altar.

The young boy positions his arms to lift himself, but cannot muster the necessary strength to get up. Instead, he raises his head slightly to see the band of fiends slowly creeping towards him.

~ My Dragon Mother: The Dragon's Cup ~

"This can't be good," Emmerich thinks to himself in a frenzied state, "but what am I supposed to do? I am too weak to fight them."

His eyes scramble across the cavern for signs of the clay bowl. If he could only drink but a small sip, he would have enough power to fend off the council and escape with his family.

"I have to get the milk," the young boy repeats beneath his breath. "One sip . . . just one sip and I can save my mother."

Summoning his last bit of strength, Emmerich struggles to get to a crawling position. Unable to completely stand, he resolves to shuffle towards his last remaining hope.

Without having to look, Emmerich can feel the approaching presence of his adversaries. The little boy sees that the deep bowl is facing upwards and is hopeful that just a tiny bit of his mother's milk remains.

Emmerich takes a deep breath and quickly scampers towards the milk-drenched wall. The young wizard then reaches for the bowl, grabbing it

~ Mother's Milk ~

firmly with both hands.

Suddenly, he feels an iron tug at his ankle and falls on his chest and face. It is Othmar and he is pulling the young boy back towards the altar, where the remaining council members await with the intent to harm him.

As the small child is dragged across the rugged terrain, Emmerich thrashes about in an effort to escape. Unable to free himself, he turns on his back and lifts the heavy bowl above his face.

All motion appears to slow as a few precious drops splash across his dry, chapped lips. Rejuvenated, Emmerich tilts the bowl forward and shakes it until every drop has been consumed.

Once at the center of the fiendish circle, the young wizard lets out a shriek unlike any he had ever made or heard before. Then, he too begins to convulse and shed his gentle demeanor. Even his eyes dim to the same abysmal tone the council members now possessed.

He screams in agony, unable to contain the raw bestial strength transferred by the unfiltered elixir. Panting in uncontrollable rage, the young boy stands amid a group of fellow fiends, one of which places its hand upon his shoulder.

"Look at us," whispers Tancred with a sinister grin. "We are the same."

"I am nothing like you," growls the deformed Emmerich, forcibly removing the chieftain's hand from his shoulder.

"Like it or not, we are an immortal family," Tancred continues. "Now, let's be rid of the malign beast that condemned us."

In a very narrow sense, Tancred is correct in highlighting their similarities. This repugnant group could, in fact, be called a sort of family in that they all had a single extraordinary thing in common -- Having drunk from a dragon!

But Emmerich had already learned that physical appearances had little to do with actually being a family. The young boy reflects on the different shapes and sizes inherent in both Herman and Leona. He further reflects fondly on the way his mother treats him and how she responds when he is

~ Mother's Milk ~

affectionate towards her.

The Bavarii are a descent people, but their council is one family that Emmerich wants nothing to do with. Without saying a word, he quickly vanishes and reappears next to his mother.

"This is my family!" he shouts, gently caressing the dragon's hide.

Emmerich notices that his mother is not moving and starts to shed a stream of tears, fearing the worst.

"She is dead!" he screams in his mind, panting furiously at the loss of his mother.

He can barely contain his anger and clenches his fist in resolution to exact his revenge.

Looking up at her executioners, the young wizard vanishes again and reappears behind Tancred; slashing him brutally on the back with his razor-sharp claws. Tancred howls in pain and futilely scurries away with Emmerich always there to catch him.

"Please stop!" cries the fallen chieftain.

But Emmerich is well beyond appeals for

mercy. His mother is gone and he will not suffer alone.

He digs his claws into Tancred and disappears with his captive, reappearing once more just below the midnight moon.

The vengeful wizard then reappears alone among the fiends, hearing Tancred scream desperately as he falls from mid air to the crater below.

One by one, the deformed wizard attacks the remaining council members, teleporting without a single villain able to see him coming. He marks them with his claws and then drops them from the height of Mount Watzmo's peak.

In the end the council members miraculously survive the fall and scatter . . . away from him . . . away from each other . . . in the primary directions of the compass.

Finally Emmerich appears before Andreas, who had been nervously watching from a distance.

"You did this!" he cries with the shrill of uncontrollable rage rushing through him.

~ Mother's Milk ~

"See what your thirst for power has done to us!" he barks at the quivering figure.

"Please forgive me," pleads a repentant Andreas, knowing that his honor had been polluted. "I did not mean for this to happen!"

"Then I won't mean for THIS to happen either," howls Emmerich, lifting his claw into the air in preparation to strike.

Suddenly, a large talon falls down upon Emmerich, pinning him to the ground below and hurling Andreas into the distance. Leona is revived and she is not ready to have her son become a killer.

"Mother . . . I thought you were dead!" he shrieks uncontrollably. "I saw what they did to you! They have to pay!"

Emmerich continues to struggle, screaming how Andreas and the council deserve to be punished. He is very strong and in her weakened condition, she doesn't have much time before he overpowers her and seals his dismal fate.

Leona lifts her right talon and rips open the flesh just beneath the claw she used to first feed him.

~ My Dragon Mother: The Dragon's Cup ~

Her blood splashes across his eyes and chin until it finally hits the mark she intended.

As the dragon's blood flows into the young boy's mouth, he sheds his ghoulish exterior and reverts to human form, slowly decreasing the heavy breathing he had developed during his fiendish state.

With Emmerich's body completely limp, Leona snatches the claw from around his neck and places it firmly in her son's mouth. She then pours her milk through the Dragon's Cup and restores his lively spirit.

The young wizard's eyes begin to glow with the same bright light that emanated from them during his initial feeding. Once again, his mother had saved him by sacrificing herself. Emmerich reaches for Leona's injured talon and strokes it in a silent display of gratitude for his salvation.

The shimmering light slowly dissipates and the young boy's eyes settle to a dark emerald green.

"Emmerich," smiles Leona, looking down at her son while gently stroking his hair. "You have my eyes."

~ Mother's Milk ~

***

A short while later, Emmerich finds his friend Claudia and introduces her to his mother. Leona thanks the young girl for helping her son and whispers an incantation into the child's right ear.

"Numquam Ieiuna" she whispers in a soft grumbling tone.

"What was that?" asks Emmerich.

"Oh, just a small spell ensuring THIS young lady will never go hungry again," his mother replies.

Claudia smiles and hugs Leona around the neck, thanking her for the divine gift.

"Climb on," Leona says, motioning to the three youths. "Let's give Claudia a ride home."

As they leave the cave, a small figure appears from behind a pile of broken pottery. It is Fulco and he has been a witness to the transformation of both Emmerich and his parents.

The boy is blind with resentment and swears vengeance against his shimmering enemy. For in his mind, Leona is ultimately responsible for turning his

~ My Dragon Mother: The Dragon's Cup ~

parents into gruesome creatures; effectively turning him into an unclaimed child . . . an orphan.

With his newfound knowledge of the dragon and the cup, he knows it is just a matter of time before such an opportunity would present itself. In the interim, Fulco resigns himself to climb down the side of the glacier and heads to his new home, the Waisenhaus.

Back at the orphanage, Claudia bids farewell to Emmerich and his family. She watches them fly towards the breaking dawn as she gnaws on a sweet batch of Heidelbeeren she had just conjured.

With the dark night behind them, Herman and Emmerich enjoy the serene rhythm of Leona's wings flapping in the cool morning breeze. They gain elevation and taper off, allowing Leona to glide for the first time in days.

Suddenly, she winces in pain and stumbles in mid air, causing her to fall and splash into the cool waters of the Königssee.

"What is it, Mother?" asks Emmerich, his voice laced heavily with concern.

~ Mother's Milk ~

"It's the council!" she says, gasping for air as she attempts to rise to the lake's surface.

The waves are extremely choppy, making it difficult for them to swim. Finally, Leona is able to match the lake's rhythm and begins to float.

Emmerich and Herman latch onto her long neck as she stabilizes her massive frame on the crystal blue water.

"One of them has taken a life," she explains, finally gaining control of her senses. "Each time that happens, I lose a bit of my own."

"That's not fair!" exclaims the young boy as they make their way towards shore.

The three of them arrive on land and sit momentarily in silence to catch their breath. It has been a trying period for all of them and there appeared to be no end in sight.

"Why is this happening to you?" asks Emmerich in a troubled tone.

"Because the Bavarii elders have drunk my milk," she says sorrowfully, "what is mine is also theirs . . . just like it is with you."

Emmerich is speechless. He knows that by feeding him, Leona's life force was split in two. Now with the council members, her spirit has been ripped an additional four times!

"What can we do mother?" Emmerich asks while caressing her cheek. "What can I do to make you better?"

"I must stop them," she says, exhaling with a cough, indicating her extreme fatigue. "If I don't reclaim my power by the setting of the Blue Moon, then I will surely perish."

"Then we'll stop them together!" Emmerich assures her while jumping to his feet.

"Herman," the young wizard calls towards the anxious gnome. "Lead the way by finding the closest one."

About the Author

Arturo Huerta lives in Houston, TX with his wife and daughter and considers them his primary source of inspiration.

When not writing fictional stories to amuse (and sometimes frighten) his friends and family, he 'delights' his neighbors by attempting to play his electric guitar on a concert grade amp.

Made in the USA
Charleston, SC
05 December 2011